NEW
RUINS

'Gripping, disturbing and compelling - it's been a while since I've read a novel so good at uncomfortable psychological accuracy, dark humour and out and out horror. I loved it.'
— Jenn Ashworth, author of *Ghosted*

'Full of existential dread and sardonic humour, I enjoyed it immensely.'
— Sharlene Teo, author of *Ponti*

'A consuming exploration of the madness of love and its distortions of the lover and the loved. A literary debut that has so much to say.'
— Adam Nevill, author of *The Ritual*

'Fresh and compelling, this claustrophobic debut will suck you in and never spit you back out.'
— Eliza Clark, author of *Boy Parts*

'This quiet novel has a wonderfully dark and savage little heart. Not only did it move me, its horror still lingers. A fantastic debut.'
— Matt Wesolowski, author of *Six Stories*

'A genuinely original novel somewhere between horror and magic realism, enviably well written, it lingers deep in the mind.'
— Ramsey Campbell

'Uncomfortable and unnerving – the best kind of blackest comedy.'
— Aliya Whiteley, author of *Skyward Inn*

A⊟SORBED

ABSORBED

KYLIE WHITEHEAD

Published by New Ruins, an imprint of Cinder House Publishing Limited.
New Ruins is a collaborative imprint between Dead Ink Books and Influx Press.
www.newruins.co.uk
@NewRuinsBooks

First edition 2021. Printed and bound in the UK by TJ Books.

Paperback ISBN: 9781838171605
Ebook ISBN: 9781838171612

Editor: Gary Budden
Copyeditor: Dan Coxon
Proofreader: Trudi Suzanne Shaw
Cover design: Luke Bird
Interior design: Vince Haig

The voice is as calm and stable as a metronome.

'He doesn't love you,' it says.

You try to push it away. You think of all the times he has told you he does. He *does* love you.

'He doesn't,' says the voice.

If only you could get deeper into him, if only you could sneak a little more of yourself into his consciousness. You want to inhabit him or have him inhabit you. He couldn't leave you if he were in you; if he *was* you.

Is it just me? Am I the only person who feels that being in love is a constant struggle to feel worthy of someone else? How am I supposed to be worthy of anyone other than myself?

I suppose I was selfish. It wasn't that I wanted him all to myself. It was that I wanted him to be a part of me; a part that I could live without – like an appendix or a pinkie toe – that couldn't live without me.

Because what's the point in loving someone if they can leave you?

ONE

The hotel was no closer to the party than our flat was. It was my idea to stay there. Owen agreed immediately. He had been doing that a lot lately.

It was New Year's Eve and we were going to a party at the shared workspace where Owen rented a desk. It was a converted warehouse in an old industrial park. He had been working there for about six months.

Everything in the hotel room was red. Owen kept jumping out from behind things: doors, curtains, corners. He wrote REDRUM across the mirror in my lipstick, mashing the tip to impotence. I wasn't even angry. I didn't think I could afford to be.

When I ironed out my face and turned towards the mirror to fix my hair, Owen flopped down on the bed to fiddle with his phone. I loved the soft patting sounds his thumbs made as they tapped on the screen, the same sounds that I woke up to each morning, safe in the knowledge that he was still there. He put the phone into a glass to amplify the sound – or perhaps to clarify it, I was never sure which – and rummaged through his backpack. He pulled out a four-pack of Red Stripe. He cracked one open and tossed the other three – bound together by the same plastic noose – onto the bed beside him. The music was jarring, and my heart wobbled to the beat.

♦

The rain was fine and misty, the kind you barely notice until it soaks through your clothes. I shielded myself with an obnoxious golf umbrella and pushed into the wind. It was warmer than I had expected, and I could feel sweat gathering on my upper lip. My make-up would be streaky by the time we arrived. My new boots were hurting in spite of the extra socks and plasters, but I didn't say anything; I didn't want Owen to know how hard I was trying. He had pulled the drawstring on his hood so tight that all I could see was his mouth, which he kept clear so he could continue to drink. He took a sip from the can and offered it to me. He was saying something about work, but I was thinking about the night ahead. He asked if I was listening. I didn't answer. He thrust the can under my nose.

'Here, you want this?' he said. I shook my head.

♦

The workspace was a low, squat building with few interior walls and plenty of exposed brick. Specks of mould and dust clung to your clothes if you happened to brush up against a wall. The people who worked there were always moaning about the shoddiness of it. 'But it's cheap,' they said. 'It's the only place I can afford.' I thought none of them could earn enough to pay rent on both a flat *and* an office, and seeing as nobody actually slept at the workspace, I expected they were propped up by parents or partners. *What luxury!* For these people, the cost of the workspace was just an excuse they could hide behind. I imagined that what they really loved was the taste of something *real*, the ability to create and own funny anecdotes about asbestos and the lack of adequate fire procedures. I pretended to despise the place. I knew it was ridiculous for me to hold onto the notion that a creative life needed to be riddled with poverty (faux or not) and misery, but the juxtaposition between that place and my office at the council, my clean and cosy flat, seemed to indicate that I was due nothing but an ordinary life. I should have been grateful for that. An ordinary life should have been all I ever wanted.

The workspace building was the largest on the site, surrounded by shacks, purposefully shabby looking to compensate for the guilt of the rich, grubby hipsters indulging in their artistic endeavours. The shacks served as studios for an ever-rotating group of creatives: furniture makers, tattoo artists, sculptors, designers of every conceivable type.

There were no curtains or blinds, and through the dripping, clouded windows I could see there was already a crush of hot bodies inside. It was only eight. I took a deep breath and forced it out through my nostrils.

I didn't want to be so down on the workspace. I knew that complaining was dull, so I attempted to revel in misery. It was all I had in terms of identity. If I couldn't be happy with my life, at least I could be entertaining in my despair. I knew plenty of men whose whole personalities revolved around being miserable bastards, and everyone loved them for it.

Owen spotted Elliott standing in a group of boys with the same kind of too-short trousers flapping around their ankles.

He pushed ahead to greet his friends and I slowed down to root through my bag for cigarettes.

Owen hugged Elliott, and when I caught up, Elliott hugged me. He held out a box of matches. I shook my head, flashing him the lighter I had clutched in my palm.

'How's it going?' he asked.

'Yeah fine,' I said, 'how're the sculptures?'

'I make furniture,' he said, without bitterness or blushing. 'Harry does the sculptures.'

I didn't really listen as Elliott proceeded to tell me about his life and art until I noticed that he wasn't speaking any more. I hadn't meant to ignore him, but I was drifting a lot at that point, struggling to focus on anyone or anything.

'Sorry, what?' I asked.

'What are you working on?' he said, and from his tone I could tell that it was not the first, or even the second, time he had asked. Owen interrupted to see if I wanted to come inside and get a drink. I said okay and followed him in. He looked over his shoulder at Elliott, relieved, as if he had been afraid of what I might say.

♦

Inside, tea lights winked and polyester shimmered. I tried not to think about the fire risk. The music was loud. Bodies packed together, tight and oily as tinned sardines. The air was close and heavy in my lungs. I tried to loosen up.

I followed Owen through the crowd – which seemed to part for him and close around me – to his desk. It had been pushed up against another desk, and the pair formed a bar. I picked up a bottle of lager and cracked it open with my lighter. I took three long slugs and looked around the room so I didn't have to burp in Owen's face. I had always gone to great lengths to disguise my bodily functions around him. He put his arm around my shoulders and kissed my head. His nose lingered in my hair. I closed my eyes and focused on the warm spot on my scalp. In moments like these, I could almost forget how much things had changed in the last few months. I tilted my face towards his and kissed him, a soft, lingering kiss that I did not want to end. But by the time I opened my eyes, he was already pulling away and opening his arms to Helena. He held her for so long that she had to pull herself out of his arms to hug me.

'Allison! It's so good to see you!' she said.

'You too,' I said, but only because I knew Owen expected it of me. He was watching closely, ready to intercept. When he saw that I wasn't going to offer any more, he asked Helena about her Christmas. She launched into a story about an uncle, a pavlova, a trip to A&E. Owen's face lit up, glowing brighter and brighter as Helena fondled her way through the story. I scanned the room and focused on pulling the corners of my tight, straight lips into something that resembled a bemused smile. I couldn't think of an excuse to leave yet. We had only been there for five minutes.

Owen was using my name too often and throwing glances in my direction. He wanted me to be friendlier, funnier, more open, more like Helena. He had not explicitly told me this, but the way he was always trying to include me was a constant reminder that I was not as approachable as he would have liked. I thought I would do anything to keep hold of him, but I just stood there not saying anything, trying desperately to smile and swigging lager like my life depended on it. Finally, he told Helena to tell me about her paintings. She looked at her feet, and the pit of anger rippled inside me. Her modesty was unbearable.

She gestured to a wall on which five pictures hung in gilt frames. The paintings were abstract, but I could tell they were supposed to be of people.

'It's just a hobby; it doesn't pay the bills,' Helena said. My eyes flickered over the price tags hanging from the frames. I supposed she didn't sell very many and I tried to quell my initial smugness. I asked her what she did for work. I knew the answer, but I had no desire to learn more about her hobby.

'I'm a set designer,' she said, 'for theatre.' When I didn't press further, she said, 'It's okay, I just wish I could carve out more space for my own art, you know?'

'Yeah,' I said, even though I didn't. I had plenty of space, but nothing of my own with which I could fill it.

I complimented the paintings as best I could. 'They're good,' I said, trying to act like I understood them. I hadn't forgotten my disdain; it just meant a lot to me that Owen did not notice the extent of it.

Satisfied that I was starting to open up, Owen turned away to talk to someone else. With a glance, he handed the conversation over to Helena, who told me that each painting was of a different feminist icon. I didn't recognise any of them.

'These women did so much for us, and most people don't even know who they are. Isn't that sad?'

I nodded, hoping she wouldn't quiz me on them. She went on. She had spent months reading about these women. She had even 'gone method'; tried to live her life as them. She had gone so far as to swap brushes, in part, for more oppressive objects, like tampons and mascara wands.

'Oh god, I'm sorry,' she said. 'Amateur, I know. I probably sound like a total idiot. Anyway, Owen says you're a writer?'

For a second, I considered the possibility that Helena and I were not that dissimilar. I let the thought die with little deliberation.

'Not really,' I said, wondering why Owen was still telling

people that. Was he disappointed by the conventional person I had become? Would he rather I was more creative, more artistic? It seemed likely.

I tried to take a sip from my bottle before I realised it was empty. I asked Helena if she wanted another drink. She sloshed the remains of her ale in front of my face and said, 'No, thanks.' I edged towards the beers.

Owen was talking to a man I didn't know about a film we had watched together recently. I stood there for a while, opening and closing my mouth, but I couldn't think of anything clever to say. Every time the words started to rise in my throat, I swallowed them down, afraid that I would embarrass Owen. I squeezed his dry palm in my clammy one and wandered outside to smoke.

◆

I didn't realise the light was on in Maggie's studio until it wasn't. She piled out wrapped in scarves, canvas bags on each arm. Gemstones dangled from her wrists and throat, attached to her body with silver chains and strings of leather. She fumbled with one of the bags while she waited for the shutters to close. I fished my cigarettes out, ready.

'Allison!' Maggie rushed over and hugged me. Hair and mangy old fake fur tickled my nose. I was so glad to see her. I held out the cigarette packet.

'You're a lifesaver.' Maggie let me light her cigarette and took a deep drag. She sighed on the exhale, smoke rolling from her nostrils.

'What's the time, what have I missed?'

'Oh, nothing. It's only nine.'

Maggie peered around me to look through the window.

'Shit, it's busy, isn't it?'

'It's New Year's.' I shrugged.

'Come on; I've got some tequila in the studio.'

I met Maggie the first time I visited Owen in the workspace, and although I knew I would oppose this move with everything I had, whether I wanted to or not, I was drawn to her instantly. I felt as though she knew my secret, knew things I had never told Owen, and because of this I felt both totally vulnerable and wholly accepted. She described herself as 'a bit psychic', and while I never believed her, I did think that she connected with something I thought I had hidden too deep to find. I had always longed for someone like this – someone who knew everything without me having to tell them, someone who would accept me anyway, no questions asked.

'Where's Julian?' I asked. Maggie's cigarette hung from her lower lip as she moved bottles and jars and brushes around in a cupboard to reveal the tequila. She was the only person I knew with a husband and child. Perhaps this was why I never felt indebted to her: she had already given so much of herself away.

'He's dropping Seren at a friend's house. He should be here in a bit. Where's Owen?'

'Inside with Helena.'

I thought I saw Maggie's eyebrow twitch, but she said nothing. She rinsed out a couple of mugs and poured generous measures of tequila into each.

Half an hour later, we locked the studio up again. I was a bit wobbly but a lot happier. Owen was standing outside talking to some of the flappy-trouser boys. Helena was laughing at something Elliott was saying. I wondered what was wrong with me. Helena was interesting, politically informed without being smug. She seemed kind, a decent balance of self-deprecating and outgoing. It wasn't her fault I was jealous.

Maybe what I really needed was a friend like her, a creative supporter to spur me on.

Owen clocked us and shouted, 'Maggie!' He reached out, touched her shoulder and kissed her cheek. His other hand fumbled around, fingers wiggling to taste the air as they found their way to my waist. He was so unassuming in that moment, naturally effervescent and full of love. I felt as if our relationship was the most natural thing in the world to him. I should have been comforted by this, but all I could think was, *Please don't leave me.*

◆

I'd always hated the countdown to midnight on New Year's Eve. Enforced fun riled me, and although other people said the same thing, I always seemed to be alone in these moments. Owen knew that I didn't want to kiss him at midnight – or rather, that I had told him I didn't – and so I couldn't blame him for not coming to look for me. I skulked around, not really speaking to anyone except to exchange a few words with Maggie and Julian each time I passed them. I smoked a lot. A few minutes before midnight, the atmosphere thickened. Everyone was drunk or high, pawing at each other and slurring. I was frightened, standing there alone in the crowd as the countdown began. I couldn't catch my breath. All around me people were hugging, linking arms and holding hands. I became trapped behind a wall of human flesh. I stood on my toes and looked around for Owen. When I spotted him, a spurt of bitter hot vomit squirted into my throat. I swallowed the thin, burning liquid and froze. Owen was standing close to Helena, head on, with one hand on her arm. She, too, had a hand on him. On the count of eight, she looked up at him, her head hanging low, her eyelashes pressed into her skull. One corner of her mouth folded into a smirk.

On six, Owen put his other hand on her other arm so that he was holding her in front of him, looking down at her. He too was smirking. I didn't start moving until three. I knocked my way through the human walls as fast as I could. On the count of one, I was spewed into them. They each raised an arm and pulled me into their hug.

Looking back, I wonder if I should have left them to it. Perhaps it would have been better if they had just kissed. I was so desperate for him not to leave me, that I could never have imagined that something much worse was to come.

TWO

It was raining again when we walked back to the hotel. I'd left my umbrella at the party, but Owen told me not to go back for it, saying he would pick it up tomorrow. I wondered if he would have said that if he didn't have a hood, but I didn't want to start a fight. I could have guessed that he would never get around to bringing it home, but I could never have imagined why. He pulled his hood tighter around his face. I swallowed my resentment; I had become used to the taste of it.

I had spent the hours after midnight lingering at the edges of the party, trying to act normal. I had sobered up, and no matter how much more I drank, I couldn't find my way back in.

Helena couldn't keep her hands off Owen. Her fingertips were constantly grazing his arm, his waist, and she kept slapping him playfully whenever she laughed. I tried not to stare, but when I looked away my thoughts swelled like a flooded river in which I was drowning. The more I thought about it, the more I came to believe that it probably wasn't just her. How many other women touched Owen like that? Was I naive to think that I was the only one? Was it wrong for me to *want* to be the only one? Owen could shake her off if he wanted, so why didn't he? Perhaps this was normal behaviour, I told myself. Elliott had his arm around his sister, and I didn't think anything was going on between them. I tried to relax. Owen and I had been together for nearly ten years. I could never decide if this made us safer or not.

♦

Sometimes, I felt like being Owen's girlfriend was the most stable identity I had ever had. I couldn't define myself by a job or a hobby. Perhaps that was why I had wanted to be a writer: it seemed likely that I was only in it for the title. I could probably define myself by my past, but I had chosen to never speak about that. Owen was my only real achievement. He was the only thing that made me worth anything, the only person who might be able to find something of real value in me. But he hadn't found it, and he was slipping away. These thoughts had been preoccupying me for some time.

At university, Owen used to laugh when I said things like, 'If we run at each other really fast, we might become one,' and, 'I love you so much, I could kill you.' I stopped saying things like that when he stopped laughing at them.

I tried to be happy for him when he found the workspace. I had long suspected that no one was really, *truly* happy for anyone else, that no one could ever see someone else's small successes and appreciate them outside the context of their own unfulfillment. I didn't think I was being uniquely selfish; in fact, I thought it was profound, as if I had uncovered something in the human condition that most people were afraid to admit. I knew he hated working at the agency, I knew he felt creatively cramped. I wanted to want more for him. His confidence had diminished over the past couple of years there. I tried hard to suppress the notion that perhaps I liked him better that way: vulnerable, miserable, like me.

He was thrilled when he found out that a desk had become available. He emailed the workspace manager right away. It was the excuse he needed to let himself go freelance. He handed in his notice at work at the end of that week. He didn't run it past me first, and once again I pretended not to be angry. I had always known that he wanted to be self-employed, someday. I just never expected that day to come. I had admired his ambition, I thought, but when he started to get the things that he had worked so hard for I began to resent him.

In those last few months he changed so much. He became more confident, more ambitious. He was dressing better; he'd made new friends. I didn't like it. The more he grew in character and confidence, the more I withered and retreated further into myself. If I was honest, I had always thought, deep down, that I was better than him in some way. As he started to carve out a place for himself, I began to lose my footing.

I really started worrying when Helena came onto the scene. I knew she wasn't at the workspace much – she only rented a desk part-time – but Owen talked about her a lot. When I first met her, I was almost relieved. She wasn't obviously gorgeous. But in the hours after our first brief meeting, my insecurity had crept in with the subtlety of a motorway pile-up. It was precisely this understated, almost imperceptible beauty – seamlessly blended with a laid-back attitude and an artistic flair – that created the aura of intellectual sex appeal that I had spent my life trying to attain. I had spent mere seconds in her presence, but it was enough for me to decide how perfect she was, how much better than me, how she could make Owen so much happier than I ever could.

Recently, Owen had been spending every Friday night at the pub with people from the workspace, Helena included. He would invite me at first, but soon stopped. It was my fault for saying 'no' so often, for staying home and sulking, for rolling away from him when he got into bed. I had stopped being grateful for his touch. I was so afraid he was going to realise how awful I was that the very feel of him repulsed me. Perhaps it's best that it happened the way it did: I would undoubtedly have driven him to her in the end otherwise.

I had been seriously considering telling him about my childhood. It wouldn't change his mind about me, but it might give him reason to pity me. How could he leave me then? About a week or so before Christmas, he told me about a conversation he'd had with Helena, about a book she was reading. I was chopping vegetables in the kitchen, my back to him as he skipped through TV channels. The words hit me like a wall of ice water. The next thing I knew, his arms were around my waist and he was asking if I was okay, a gentle laugh in his voice. He didn't seem concerned that I could have sliced my fingers off.

'I must have zoned out,' I said and forced myself to laugh along with him. I tried to ignore the subject he had raised, and talked about the soup I was making until he forgot what he had been telling me.

At first, I imagined I would tell him someday, but suddenly we had been together for ten years. At that point, revealing secrets from my past seemed insulting. But after he brought it up, directly, I felt I no longer had an excuse for keeping my secret. It was starting to feel like I was living a lie. I never did tell him, though; I just incubated the guilt.

◆

I didn't think the party had been quite as disastrous as it could have been. I had been so worried about seeing Helena, about seeing Owen with her, but nothing had happened. Surely they hadn't been about to kiss. I was paranoid. I tried to grasp for whatever I had felt when I saw Helena outside the workspace – smoking, and warm-faced like an old friend – but it was gone.

◆

I was limping by the time we got back to the hotel. Owen kept putting his arm around my waist like he was trying to steady me. I guess he thought I was drunk. When we got back, the hotel was locked for the night. We had to ring the doorbell. An old woman with patchy dyed-orange hair took her time coming to the door. We could hear her fumbling with the lock on the inside. We giggled. When she opened the door, we could smell the sweet, rotten alcohol on her breath, sweating from her skin. She hugged us both. Owen answered all her questions about the party. When there was a break, he said, 'Right then,' and the woman said, 'Oh, yes of course.' We went up the stairs while she tottered off down the hall. We could hear her television after she shut the door.

I was rooting around in my bag for a few minutes before Owen realised he had the key. We were laughing so hard by then that I had to keep flexing my pelvic floor, so I didn't wet myself.

'I'm going to peeeee!' I whispered, both of us laughing hard, tears brimming in our eyes. It was like something had finally broken between us, as if the past six months had been building up to this: Owen and I, bringing in the new year together, very much in love. When we got into the room, he shrugged off his dripping coat and started to fumble with his shirt buttons. I got a towel from the bathroom and when I handed it to him, he pulled me down onto the bed.

The bed was a stupid mahogany four-poster, matching the fake mahogany cladding on the lower half of the walls. The bedspread was the same deep, velvety red as the wallpaper and the carpet. I imagined that the upholstery had once been white, the wood maple. Drenched in blood. Flashes of violence were not uncommon for me, not since I found out where I had come from. I shook the thought away. This was not the time.

Owen threw the red quilted pillows onto the floor. We got tangled in the bedspread as we tried to separate absurd layers of sheets. It was then that I decided it would be a good time for the lingerie.

I knew that relationships were understood to transcend lust over time, although I could never understand why that would be something to aspire to. I thought that it was my responsibility to keep our sex life going. It seemed vital, that without sex he would get bored of me, would realise how little I had to offer. But more recently, frequency alone had not felt enough. I knew that I needed to up my game if I wanted to keep his interest. That was when I decided that the lingerie would be a good idea. I hadn't worn anything that didn't come as part of a Marks and Spencer multipack, that wasn't one hundred per cent cotton, in years. I hadn't meant to stop trying; I just forgot. And so I shopped around until I found something I didn't feel ridiculous wearing. Something I thought might renew his excitement about me, about us. I had felt stupid at the thought of putting it on before the party, but I felt braver now. I must have been a little drunk.

I pulled away from Owen, told him I was going to have a shower to warm up, and ran into the bathroom. I washed quickly without getting my face or hair wet, rubbing shower gel vigorously between my legs even though I knew I shouldn't. I touched up my make-up and put the underwear on. *At least I am clean. At least he is drunk.*

Owen looked surprised when I emerged from the bathroom. I couldn't tell if he was excited or disgusted. The horror I felt at the thought of his repulsion was physical, like my organs had become entangled in my skin; I felt hollow and heavy and bloody and hot. In the bathroom, I had swallowed the possibility of his disgust – it was melodramatic, even for me – and yet here it was. His lips parted as if his own horror was forcing its way out, but apart from that he froze, a terrified animal unsure of its next move. But slowly, his face folded upwards into a lazy grin. The flash of his crooked front teeth flooded me with a heat that sent me rushing into his arms. He pulled me close and kissed the lines around my eyes, the marionette's grooves between my nose and mouth, the blank spaces where my ears ended before my cheeks began. He kissed my stomach and my thighs, and I felt the impressions his lips left in my flesh. I was grateful for the physical impact his body had on my own; his influence was intoxicating, and I wilted into it. His eyes were dark but warm and he pushed my hands down into the sheets. I was trapped beneath his weight. It was comforting to be at his mercy. He dug the tips of his fingers into my wrists and already I felt the penny bruises blooming on my skin. He told me I was beautiful, and I believed him as I only did when we were fucking. I pushed myself on top of him, tucking my stomach, performing. I pressed my forehead into his and bucked my hips down as hard as I could. I was grinding onto him, pressing my face into his, when I began to feel that I was sinking. *It is finally happening*, I remember thinking, *we are becoming one*. I wasn't scared, but Owen was.

I looked down for his hands where they should have been resting on my hips, but I could see only the stumps of his wrists as they sunk into my flesh. I tried to pull my face away from his, but our foreheads had become welded together. My hands fused with his chest. His body grew smaller and more distant as he oozed into me. I can still remember the fear I saw in his eyes as I absorbed him. And then all I could see was a dark, velvety red. I don't know if it was the bed sheets or the insides of my eyelids.

TH—REE

I walked my fingers through the space his body should have occupied. The night only half unfolded itself. I couldn't yet see what was at its centre, could not understand why I had woken up alone. I pictured Owen waking early, going out for some reason. Did he leave?

It wasn't until I stumbled into the bathroom that I recalled his face as I consumed him. I looked in the mirror, bugged out my eyes and pulled my lips apart, first into a snarl and then into a silent scream. Over the last decade, I had taken a lot of Owen into myself, including many of his mannerisms. I would pick up phrases he had picked up elsewhere, I'd fold his opinions into my own. Sometimes I would stand before the mirror in the toilets at work, contorting my face into expressions I had learned from him. But this was different. I didn't look like Owen in the mirror.

I *was* him. I held the frozen scream for a long time. I stared at my throat in the mirror, running my fingers over the knob of my larynx and squinting to see past my tonsils. When I tried to relax my face, I couldn't. My expression was stiff. I was stuck. I massaged my cheeks with my fingers, and slowly, I began to look like myself again. I switched on the shower. I didn't close the bathroom door.

I can't explain why I carried on as I did. It was like somebody had pushed me, and the momentum alone was carrying me through the motions. Although I could remember it, I couldn't comprehend what had happened. If I could, I'm sure I would have realised the absurdity of it. I would have panicked. Instead, I brushed my teeth. I let the electric toothbrush roam over my gums, watching my face in the mirror for more signs of Owen. I stepped into the shower and massaged the watery, wet-dog-scented hotel shampoo into my hair. I dug my fingernails into my scalp as if, by breaking the skin, the shampoo could seep into my blood and clean me from within. As I was rubbing shower gel into my skin, something hardened inside me. My hands dropped instinctively to my stomach. I crumpled. The pain was sharp and constant like a cramp. I howled until my mouth filled with water and I had to spit. The pain came alive and I thought then that I could feel Owen physically inside me; fighting to escape or clinging to my insides. My hand was drawn between my legs, as if independent of me. There I found a loose, smooth moisture, slipperier than the wetness of the shower, thicker than the suds of the shower gel. I pulled the shower head down and angled it between my thighs.

Afterwards, I sat on the bed wrapped in a towel. My hair was dripping. Tears and snot and shower water dribbled down my chin and dripped onto the sheets. I was still sobbing when I heard a knock at the door. It was the hotel owner, the same woman that Owen and I had mocked so openly the night before. She was not merry any more. I made eye contact and cried harder, not hiding my sorrow or wiping the gunk away. She looked me up and down and asked me to leave. I was still sobbing in big, wet gasps when she turned and walked down the corridor. I didn't shut the door or dry my hair. I put my dirty underwear back on (the full pants, not the lingerie), and my dress from the previous night. I shoved all of my things into my backpack and all of Owen's into his, as if that mattered now, as if we would ever be distinguishable from one another again. I dropped the key with a heavy *plink* onto the reception desk, hoping it would scratch the fake mahogany, and began the walk home.

The rain had turned to ice, and I waddled ridiculously, a grossly dolled-up donkey with a backpack on each shoulder. I curled my toes in my boots to stop the rubbing, but I could already feel the wet slime of burst blisters seeping through my tights. I wondered if pus could freeze. *Perhaps Owen will be waiting at home*, I thought, but I didn't believe it. The grass glistened white and the sky shimmered a murky green and I wondered if the whole world had flipped. A passing bus carved the sun from the sky and flung it at my face. Everything felt like a personal attack.

Sunlight slashed the dull fabric of darkness, exposing the dust that glittered into life at the sound of my key in the door. The objects inside the flat held little comfort in themselves, and to be surrounded by them again filled me with a sense of both belonging and unbridled loneliness. My ears and teeth ached from the cold.

I dragged my fingertips along the wall as I walked, something I had always done in an attempt to feel something, anything, in response to my surroundings.

◆

For Owen's birthday two years earlier, we had gone on holiday to Barcelona. As we wandered around the city, I counted my complaints in my head, trying to ration them so I wouldn't seem ungrateful. I gripped Owen's arm, picking at and preening him. When I spoke, my voice oozed out like pus, strained and bitter. Owen had little to say. He seemed content in the hot silence, oblivious to my anxiety. As our relationship grew, silence became a bigger and bigger part of it. Unlike me, Owen didn't seem to be afraid that it would one day swallow us both down into two separate bellies. I could never think of anything good enough to say to him, so I complained, and then I worried that my complaints would drive him away.

Owen insisted that we visit an art museum and I said yes. What if he could see me, pensive and serene, my shoes clopping cleanly as I submerged myself in the art, studying paintings and photographs, ceramics and sculptures like they were speaking to me, as if they had something to say that only I could understand? What if Owen could see the tilt of my head, watch as my lips parted in response to an image I needed to connect with more closely? What if he thought I could get anything from this experience at all? Would he love me then, as I loved him?

I had only taken a few steps inside the gallery before I realised I was losing him. I had moved on too quickly, and he had wandered away from me. Did he know he was doing it? Was he *trying* to lose me? I could feel myself slipping, falling, floundering towards the floor. I felt dizzy and my tears blurred the art. All around me sculptures leered, laughing at me. They too knew that I would lose Owen to something he found altogether more beautiful than me. How would he still be able to love me if he found out that I could not see beauty in anything but him?

I roamed the gallery on my own, my love strengthened by the fear of losing him.

I was sure that the holiday would be the end for us. I knew that love was not a guarantee of entertainment; I owed Owen nothing. I was being melodramatic. So why did I feel like this?

Later that afternoon we sat on the beach. Owen had his eyes closed, and I looked out at the sea, wondering what he was thinking about. Waves rolled towards us and smashed like glass onto the beach. Wasn't sand the same as glass anyway? Wasn't I also falling to pieces there on that beach? Beside me a child dug a hole with a plastic spade, while his mother lay topless and wrinkled and still as a corpse beside him. I tried to say something to Owen, but he was wearing earphones and couldn't hear me. I stroked his arm, but he didn't stir. I walked out to sea.

The cold water scratched my toes as I waded in. I kept my eyes on the sand bed, watching for crabs and jellyfish. The sun burned my eyes and scalp as my feet froze beneath the surface. I took a deep breath and thrust myself down into the cold, salty water, holding my head under until my lungs were hot, stinging balloons exploding in my chest. When I popped up, gasping and squinting the salt from my eyes, an old man stumbled in the water and looked at me questioningly. I smiled as if to reassure him that I was neither drowning nor attempting a futile suicide in the shallows. He frowned and turned to walk away, his yellow Speedos rising like the sun against the horizon. I watched as a woman of roasted leather handed him a towel while he turned back to glare at me. I waved cruelly and turned around to walk further into the sea. When the water reached my waist, I lay on my back and waited for the current to carry me far away. Nothing happened. I paddled back to shore.

♦

I waded through the viscous air of the neglected flat, picking up things that Owen had used regularly. I thumbed the bristles of his toothbrush; ran the bread knife over the tip of my forefinger; stroked the cushion that he always said was too itchy. Perhaps these objects were magnetic. Maybe, somehow, their mundanity could draw him out.

I paused in front of a charity shop oil painting that hung on the chimney breast. Owen had bought it. I had never known what he loved about the scene: a wooden shack beside a lake, pines looming like vengeful spirits. I looked carefully for the first time to try to understand it. I took one step, two steps, three steps towards the painting until the tip of my nose was an inch from the canvas. I tried to focus on one pine, to feel its motion, to smell its cool, fresh needles. The trees began to sway. In the window of the shack I could see a small, pale face. Owen? I tried to look away, but whichever way I turned my head I could still see the face glaring at me.

There was a breeze and I could hear the muted shush of the wind slinking through the pines. The sound was disjointed, out of sync with the scene; the rhythm of the trees' movements, divorced from the sound of wind whipping through the branches. The air was cold, and it tickled my nostrils. My breath clouded out in front of me; my soul expelled. The world I was in belonged to Owen. He had chosen it and he had chosen me.

The air rippled like water as I moved through it, sending out waves that ruffled the trees and skimmed the lake. The sounds around me came into focus, the wind howling, colliding with my movements. I swam through the thick, cold air towards the house, which I approached at a steady pace, no matter how fast I moved my feet and legs. The scent was now of Owen's body, his sweat, our combined scent, the smell of our sex. It darkened as the warm sense of him rose up and away from me. A clap of thunder ushered me into the shack, and the sky began to fall wetly as I shut the door behind me.

◆

Often, when he kissed me, he would lean in too far, as if he wanted to press himself through me. I would have to tilt my head back to accommodate him. Sometimes I would laugh and nuzzle him back with my forehead. He would laugh too and apologise and kiss me again. I just wanted to be kissing him. How did it come to this?

◆

I sat on the bed. I didn't take off my shoes or gloves or coat. I sank my face into the pillow, pulled the top of the duvet – the part that I was certain Owen would have held closest to his mouth as he slept – to my face. I couldn't smell him. Everything smelled of nothing.

As my eyes grew heavy and my head grew light, I realised that perhaps now there was nothing left to fear, that everything I wanted was within me. I was in love, but love was free to mean something different now. I didn't love myself as such, but I felt my love internally, as if I were also on the receiving end of it. It came from and arrived at the same place, so that I was simultaneously loving and loved.

The completed circuit buzzed and everything I had once thought I knew about love burned violently. After what had happened with my birth parents, I'd learned that the autonomy of people was problematic. I had learned never to expect another's love, and without that expectation I had never developed acceptance. When I fell for Owen (and I could not have fallen any harder), I knew that neither the quantity nor quality of love could guarantee my security. Love was not built to last, and people were not built to love.

And yet.

Why had this happened to me?

F—OUR

The weekend passed in a fever dream, endless eventualities spinning through my head between cold, sticky naps. At some point I had taken my dress off and put one of Owen's dirty T-shirts on. In snatches of consciousness I stared at the front door, half-expecting him to come bursting through it, laughing at my greasy hair and stale breath before pulling me into his arms, soothing me like a baby.

I didn't make a conscious effort to carry on as normal, but when my alarm went off on Monday morning, I showered and dressed and walked to work, as if doing so was the only option.

◆

I dragged my feet through the swirling brown bog of carpet. Jean sighed when I dropped my bag on my desk. The position of her eyebrows told me I was late. Jean wasn't my boss, but she liked to think that her age and passion for local government made her superior to me. I didn't question her superiority. She deserved to be my boss, and we both knew that she never would be.

Before I sat down, the photo of Owen that I had stuck to the frame of my monitor fell and landed face down on my desk. It was a passport photo, Owen's face pale and flat. I remember how hungover he was that day. I tried to remember how annoyed I was that he had got drunk without me. Usually the memory of a fight was enough to make me angry again, but as I stared at the photo, I could not summon the pain I must have felt.

I picked the Blu-Tack from the back of the photo. I rolled it between my thumb and forefinger like a nipple and absently stuck the photo back on the monitor frame. Owen glared out at me and my heart beat harder and faster, as if it was trying to escape. As I stared at the photo my eyes blurred and my head buzzed. It was like Owen was nudging me from the inside, trying to make room for himself. I ripped the photo off the monitor and gulped down stale office air. I could almost hear Jean's eyebrows shift. I dropped behind the monitor where she couldn't see me and stuffed the photo in the in tray. I was shaking, but I didn't feel scared. He was there. He was all mine.

◆

After I graduated, I took a job selling refurbished power tools. The shop was in an old warehouse, more like a dilapidated barn than the workspace where Owen ended up. I sat behind the counter all day with a black-and-white portable television, ringing up lawn mowers and drills and all sorts of electrical saws. I thought that I would focus on writing. That was when I still thought I had something important to say. Before I realised that all of my opinions were insubstantial; not wrong exactly, just ill-informed.

I was happy in the shop, I think, for a while at least. I look back on those first months as the happiest of my life. It felt like the beginning of something. My best friend, Natalie, who I had known since college, had just taken an unpaid internship at a publishing house and spent most of her days photocopying and making coffee. It sounded exciting – working in publishing – but I felt that my path was nobler somehow: working for minimum wage, bootstrapping my writing career. We used to talk about how Natalie would publish my book one day. It had been years since we last talked about that.

The summer folded into winter. I can't say it went quickly, but time passed with such ease that I didn't notice. Owen was doing well. He didn't love his job, but he had been promoted, and it was hard for me to imagine him being unhappy with the salary and superiority his work afforded him. I was afraid to admit that I felt uneasy with him doing well, so much better than I was. I started looking for something that would pay me a bit more, something that would make me more equal to him. I lied a bit on my CV, and I got a job in housing at the council.

It worked at first. I convinced myself that I was helping people. When I talked about what I did, my friends would say how important it was, and I would brush them off. I would say that I just wanted to do something useful, that it seemed selfish doing easy work while I focused on my writing, that this way I could do both. That was six years ago. I realised I hated my job within the first six hours. I had always thought that knowledge would make me stronger, but I learned quickly that ignorance really *was* bliss. I learned about homelessness assessments, about the kind of person who deserved a home, and the kind of person who didn't. I learned that there was a simple solution to homelessness, and that it just never happened.

I heard gruesome stories about hoarders and decay, overdoses and abuse. The longer I stayed, the heavier I felt. The nicotine-coloured suspended-cardboard ceiling was like a giant thumb, pushing me down into the quicksand carpet. Every evening, as I walked home, the familiar route reminded me that I would need to come back again tomorrow, and every other day, just to survive. I felt bad for the people who got lost in the system, but I was afraid of them, of how close I was to them. The constant fear of the world being pulled out from underneath me was too much to bear. I didn't feel too guilty about hating my job. I was only in admin.

I had started sinking long before New Year's Eve. Everyone around me was succeeding in some way, growing up. I was trapped. I thought that Owen was all I had. I didn't believe other people when they said they felt the same as I did, as if our malaise was somehow comparable because we were of a similar age.

◆

I stared at the remnants of the Blu-Tack on the monitor while I composed my thoughts. I wondered what it would be like to have a job that I could get lost in. Owen would get so engrossed in his work that he couldn't even look at his phone. I couldn't imagine ever being that busy, but I opened my emails and tried.

I was successfully engrossed in work until Jean jumped up, and the look on her face told me that our manager was nearby. Darren wasn't much older than me, but he still felt like a creepy uncle: genuinely interested in my personal development while unable to stop looking at my chest.

Darren wished the whole office a happy New Year. His voice did nothing to help his professional demeanour. He sounded like he had been involved in a horrific and unfortunate helium-prank accident, which seemed the exact sort of thing that might happen to him. Jean was fawning, rubbing her hands together nervously and then waving her arms around like a mad clown. She was attempting to hug Darren but chickened out at the last minute. A little grunting noise slipped out of me, almost a laugh. I had never thought my feelings about Darren and Jean were particularly cruel, but for the first time I felt guilty as they both looked down at me cock-headed. I offered up my best seasonal greeting, but my voice came out thick and wet like I was about to throw up.

Jean asked Darren for 'a word' and ushered him into a corner before he could respond, her hand hovering over his arm without quite touching it. *Is it that obvious that I am no longer who I was? What if the only person who really 'gets' me is Jean?*

I pitied Jean when I first met her. I would find out later that she was around fifteen years older than me, but she seemed much older, as if she had given up. She was always on some kind of diet and she'd always say it was for a medical reason – allergies or digestive issues – which made me feel uncomfortable. I didn't need to know so much about her gut health. I was embarrassed that she would talk about it so freely. I would have respected her more if she admitted she was just trying to lose weight: we all wanted to be better versions of ourselves. I knew that Jean was single, she had been for the whole time I had known her. Maybe she had never been loved. She didn't socialise much, although she did the occasional evening class. She never talked about dates or relationships, but she would blush over delivery boys and young men from other departments. I had always found her loneliness creepy and sad.

I'm not sure when I stopped feeling sorry for Jean and started disliking her instead. At first her pathos was almost endearing, but at some point it started to feel manipulative and contagious.

If I accepted Jean, I would risk becoming like her. I reasoned that if I let her get too close, she would tear me apart.

Owen would always laugh at my anecdotes about Jean, but later he'd find light-hearted ways to make me feel guilty about how I thought of her. She wasn't a *bad* person; she didn't deserve my hostility. I had always been aware of this in a vague way, but that morning, with Owen bubbling through my veins, I took on a new perspective: Owen's perspective. I didn't suddenly like Jean, but I felt more tolerant of her, accepted her as a separate being who needn't have any influence in my life. It wasn't the same as empathy, it was more that I simply accepted her ways without questioning them. It was exactly the sort of small detail I had always envied in Owen but was never able to replicate.

A slat of sun squeezed through a gap in the blinds and burned a bright stripe into my monitor all morning. I couldn't be bothered to jiggle the blinds, so I dragged all my windows to the other side of the screen. It was late morning when Darren popped up behind me asking for 'a chat'. I set my computer to sleep so no one could access it without my password. I got up without saying anything and followed Darren into the meeting room.

Darren was new in the office, not *new* new, but he had been the most recent to join. Turnaround wasn't high in our department and it seemed likely that most people would work there until they retired or died. Darren had taken a special interest in me straight away. I'd immediately clocked him as a creepy guy, but I was only unsettled when I thought I'd figured out why he cared so much. I used to keep notes about my birth parents in my email drafts. Whatever I could find about them I would save and read obsessively, over and over. I had never revealed anything about my past to anyone, but the evidence was there for the taking. It was a long time until it occurred to me that perhaps Darren knew. Surely he could access my email account. Was he now the only person who knew the truth about me, a truth I had hidden from everyone, regardless of how much I loved them? It angered me that Darren should be the only one to know. I lay awake for whole nights, my stomach a loose bag of worms, panicking over how I could tell it all to Owen. Was omitting the truth the same as lying?

How much of myself did I need to give to him, for him to give me everything he had? As it happened, not that much.

Darren asked if I wanted to get a cup of tea. There was a time when I would have expected the worst, but as I sat there I felt calm, confident in my abilities as an employee. I said no to the tea. He shuffled some papers that I knew he didn't need.

'How are you?' he said. His eyes were milky and slitty like a snake's.

'Yeah, good,' I said. 'You?'

Could he see Owen inside me? Could he tell there was something different and knew what I had done? Was he going to report me to the police? If he did, what would he say? What evidence did he have – what evidence could anyone have – that I had consumed my boyfriend? In a way, it was the perfect crime. I pressed my lips together to stop a sick smile from slipping out.

'Really great, thanks for asking. I'm so excited about this year, you know?'

I half nodded, lowering my head but not lifting it again. Darren took a breath, opened his mouth and paused. I held my hands together and waited.

'Allison, I think you've shown some really great potential here, and I just want you to know, I'm really rooting for you. I really think this year is going to be your year, you know? I need someone to help me run the show, and I really think that person could be you if you just… applied yourself a bit more.'

'What about Jean?' I asked.

'Oh, Jean's great,' he said, 'but between you and me, I just don't think she's really got what it takes. Anyway, she's happy where she is, you know what I mean?'

I didn't think much of Jean, but I knew Darren was not referring to her ability to do the job, but to her age. Jean was not old, but she was too old for people to consider giving her new opportunities. I wondered when people had started thinking that Jean was past it. I knew I had always thought it. I hadn't necessarily equated it with age, but with her general haplessness. There must have been a time when Jean's whole life stretched out ahead of her. Did she realise that she was at the end of the road? I wondered when I would be past it. Perhaps I already was.

I should have called him out, should have told him that his boss was almost twenty years older than Jean, that it was not okay that she should be overlooked because she was a woman. I had always put a lot of energy into hating Jean, but now I could see that she worked hard, she was loyal, she deserved better. But I didn't say any of that. I just said, 'Yeah, cool.'

'Look,' Darren was trying to get real with me, 'performance reviews are in March, and I'm going to put you forward for a supervisor role. I think I can make a good case for you, I just need you to work with me, okay?'

'Sure,' I said. I *would* be a good supervisor if I applied myself, but I didn't want it.

Darren sighed and smiled. I couldn't tell if he was relieved or frustrated. Either way, the conversation was over, and he had seemingly teleported to the door, which he held open to let me out.

Something I had always found confusing was why people expected so much of me. Everyone expected me to try harder, do better. Didn't they know that I was already doing my best? Didn't they see how insulting they were being?

Back at my desk I opened a new document and started to write my letter of resignation. Owen had told me repeatedly that I should just quit my job if it made me so unhappy, but we both knew that wasn't really an option.

'You'll find another job,' he would say, and then, when I started looking, he'd say, 'There's no need to rush, you should wait for the right job.' He never understood the urgency with which I needed to make decisions, the impossibility of waiting around to kick-start my life.

I felt calm and in control as I tapped out my resignation. It was soothing, making plans. It was the reason I had notebooks in which I had scrawled suicide notes; just acknowledging my options felt productive. A tingling rush of warmth spread through my body, and I let Owen's words pour from my fingertips. Maybe this was what it felt like to be happy for someone. Perhaps this was what it felt like to be Owen.

FIVE

When I got home, I put the news on. There had been a massacre somewhere, the same clips reeling over and over: white sheets, bloodstains, children crying, lights flashing. I sat there and watched the images until I might as well have been staring at a screensaver. In a way it was soothing, all that chaos and violence: it was not mine. What I didn't notice at the time was how little guilt I felt at my own reaction to the tragedy. It was sad, but I didn't dwell on the effect it had on me, or rather the lack of effect. Something terrible had happened in the world, but it wasn't my fault, and for the first time I realised that I did not deserve to carry the weight of it to be valid. It wasn't that I didn't care; it was more that my caring was less selfish now. Removing myself from what I saw on the television, I was able to feel empathy and sorrow without worrying if my reaction was adequate.

With Owen I had always felt that I was performing what it was I wanted him to see, but now I realised that my preoccupation with his perception of me was – in part – what had obstructed the connection I thought we were supposed to have. We had eaten dinner while hurricanes raged across the ocean, we had read breaking news alerts of terrorist attacks in countries we had never heard of. But instead of opening myself up to emotion and education, I had focused solely on how other people perceived me.

The flat felt lacking without Owen in it, as if the nature of his body had made the atmosphere breathable. I felt that he was present, but his presence wasn't physical. It was louder without him there to soak up the dead air. I turned the television off, and because I didn't know what else to do, I just stood in the middle of the room for a while.

A sharp pain squealed into my head. The sound was like that of the handbrake turns Owen would do when he took me out to practise driving. I never did pass my test. I took a second to realise that the squealing sound was the phone, and a second more to remember where it was; no one had rung the landline for years. I found it under a blanket and picked up the smooth, cold Bakelite receiver. I was only wearing one shoe. I didn't know why or when I had taken the other one off. It was nowhere to be seen.

'Hello?' I answered, but there was no voice at the other end, just the buzzing insect of the dial tone. I wondered if the phone had really rung, but I could still feel the shrill echo ricocheting through my skull. The rain on the windows and door sounded like a thousand tiny fists knocking to come in. My skin was heavy, as if it was about to slide off my skeleton. I could feel Owen all over me, dragging me down like quicksand. The light fitting was swinging gently. There was a breeze. The window was open, and I was certain I hadn't opened it. Owen would always open the windows at night when our legs were glued together with sweat. But I liked it, the gluing, and I kept the window closed when I could. I pulled it shut and pushed myself towards the ceiling with my toes. My fingertips grazed the paper lampshade. The air was cold and thick like ice cream, and I sliced it with the arcs of my arms as I lowered them to my sides.

I heard a noise from somewhere, but it was either too quiet or too short to decipher. A pair of Owen's trainers, not the ones he had been wearing the other night, were lying just inside the bedroom. Had they been there before I went to work? He sometimes left them there when he came home drunk, but he would always put them away in the morning. He was weird about his shoes. One time, he had lined them up in order of colour by the front door, and since then, he had always put each pair back in the exact slot from which he had taken it. I turned from the stairs to the door. There were two gaps in the shoe line. One of the missing pairs was his favourite, the pair he had worn on New Year's Eve. He had bought them a few weeks earlier, and I had called them ugly and pretentious. I knew exactly where they were now. I had shoved them into his backpack when I left the hotel, and the backpack was now stuffed underneath our bed, out of sight. But the other pair, the pair at the bottom of the stairs, those were his everyday trainers.

I took off around the flat, picking up as much speed as the cramped layout allowed. I burst into the bathroom, the office, the airing cupboard. Each time I flung a door open, I expected to see him there, eyes wide and questioning, wondering why I was acting crazy. But I was alone, running around my flat and slamming doors like a person possessed.

I trudged back to the bedroom, picked up the trainers, and threw them back into the wrong slot. I thought that pissing him off might somehow bring him out of me, but my thoughts were incoherent. I was upset and angry, but I didn't know if the anger I felt was mine or his.

The phone rang again, and I glared at it. Was it really ringing this time? I picked it up and waited, not saying anything. But there was someone there. The call went something like this:

'Hello?' A woman's voice at the other end. 'Owen, are you there?'

'Hi, Phillipa.' I wasn't sure if I would have preferred another frightening hoax call over Owen's mother. 'Owen's... not here.' I didn't know what else I could say, but I somehow expected her to understand.

'Oh, I just wanted to wish you both a late happy New Year! Did you go out in the end?' It wasn't uncommon for Phillipa to call late with her regards.

'Yeah,' I said.

'Lovely, did you do anything nice?'

'Just a party.'

'Lovely,' repeated Phillipa.

'Owen's gone!' I spat the words out and winced. I was so sure of what had happened but had been desperately hoping I was wrong. A part of me expected that Owen was out there somewhere, not deep inside me. He had been 'gone' for almost a week, and I had just discovered another place that he certainly was not. He hadn't gone back to his mother. Where else could he have gone? It was becoming more and more difficult to convince myself – in the times I most needed comfort – that I had not absorbed him.

'Oh, don't worry dear,' Phillipa said, 'I just wanted to check on you both, you see—'

'No, he's gone,' I whined, more insistent now, 'I don't know where he is. You haven't heard from him?'

'No.' She paused. 'I haven't. When did you last see him?'

'New Year's Eve.'

'Well, what happened?'

'I just woke up, and he was gone.'

'Oh Allison, darling, I'm so sorry.'

I couldn't say anything. Why didn't Philippa care that her son was missing? But this was textbook Philippa. Literally phoning in her faux concern.

'Look, I'll find out where he is and get him to call you, okay?' she said after a pause.

'How will you—'

'Take care of yourself, dear.'

The dial tone.

For the first time I really began to consider the logistics of the problem. When would Owen's mother start to worry? How much time did I have?

◆

I was barely listening when Owen started to tell me about his Aunt Emily. We'd had a couple of pints and he'd been talking about his course or the shop where he worked part-time. It wasn't that I was uninterested in what he was saying, but I was preoccupied with something too unimportant to recall later.

'She was basically my mum,' he said, out of nowhere.

We had been together for perhaps a year and a half. We were living in a house with five other students. We each had our own bedroom; it made the commitment seem less, somehow. I longed to know Owen at the most intimate level, to know everything about him, even though it terrified me. But whenever he told me anything about his past, I felt sick. I was horrified that he had lived before he met me, that he had existed in the world as a person I would never know. There were people, ex-girlfriends, old school friends, who knew him better than I did, and this made me feel so vulnerable that I would start to sweat and shake. I knew that how I felt was unacceptable, so I tried to act normal; I couldn't afford for him to start withholding things from me. I didn't think about how unfair that was. I had different rules for each of us.

He told me how he moved in with Aunt Emily after college. She had cancer; he didn't say which kind, and I thought it was the kind of question you could never ask. Besides, I had never known cancer, and I was not ready to get acquainted. I remember the way his eyes started to fog over. I didn't know if he was retreating into some darkness inside, or if he was simply on the verge of tears. I hadn't seen him cry then, and I wasn't sure I was ready to. I would not see that darkness in him again, until I absorbed him.

He said that Emily needed some help around the house, that he'd spent a lot of time there in his childhood anyway, probably more than at his own home. He never explained why. Every time I met Phillipa, I tried to figure out what was wrong with her, but apart from being a little vague and dopey, I never did. She must have been absent in some way, but I never got the details.

In spite of the darkness in his eyes, he spoke fondly of those years with his aunt. He'd done a couple of design internships and he was grateful he'd had that opportunity. She'd taught him how to play bridge, and he'd spent every Wednesday night sat in the kitchen with her and two of her friends whose names I can't remember. She really wanted him to make something of himself, he said. She was the only person who had made him feel that he could *be* someone. I remember how it felt when he said that: a punch in the gut. He smiled. I remember the awareness I felt of my own face, aware that I needed it to look sympathetic, to look like I couldn't empathise with loss like that, but that I was open to helping him heal. I remember taking a sip of my drink, how it went down wrong, how I convulsed on a gag. Owen looked at me, but he didn't really see. For a while, he didn't say anything. It was like he had finished the story, but he couldn't have. I knew the ending, but I decided he wanted me to ask for it. I realised later that I was right: sometimes it's better to end your story so that you can begin a new one.

'So that's when you applied?' I asked. 'For uni?'

Not at first, he said. He waited for a few months, then applied through clearing in the summer. I thought about the unopened boxes I'd seen stacked in his room the first night we'd met. I thought, *How much of his dead aunt does he lug around with him?* How could I even begin to compete for that place in his heart? It was a horrible thought and I tried to ignore it.

'The worst thing is…' he said, and I braced myself, 'they didn't even tell me until after the funeral. Apparently, she told Mum not to bother me, to let me 'settle in'. She wanted me to get good grades, you know? I didn't even get to tell her that none of it even matters in the first year.'

How *could* I have told him about my birth parents? He had already seen the woman in whom he'd placed almost everything crumble away. He had experienced his own pain and did not need to be burdened with mine.

◆

Another week passed with no sign of Owen's return. Every day I went to work, came home and lay on the sofa watching the front door, trying to think up a plan. I was torn between trying to get him out, trying to cover up what had happened, accepting the whole thing and trying to move on, or asking for help. But who could help with something like this? And what would I say when people started to ask questions? Owen's mother hadn't called back. None of his friends had asked me where he was. But sometime soon, someone was going to want to find him. And I was going to have think of something to say.

◆

About two weeks into the new year, I woke up in the middle of the night with the weight of Owen's arm pressing me into the mattress. I tried to roll over, but I couldn't move. I was frightened before I even remembered that he was gone. I rolled my eyes around the room, straining them so hard in their sockets that they ached. A figure loomed by the door. I closed my eyes and squeezed them tight, tried to focus, tried to breathe. Out of the darkness behind my closed eyes came Owen's face, that contorted scream I remembered from New Year's Eve. I couldn't shout out; I didn't even know if I was breathing. It felt like hours that I lay there, staring into his pained eyes, destroying him over and over again, sweating and shaking and unable to move. Finally, I realised that my fists were clenching and unclenching, and then I realised that I could move again. I flung myself onto Owen's side of the bed. The figure by the door was just our dressing gowns sharing a hook. I lay awake the rest of the night hugging his pillow.

SIX

I hadn't tried to *do* anything about Owen because I didn't feel as if he had gone anywhere. I understood that I had absorbed him, but I wasn't lonely. I missed his touch and the sound of his voice, but these things seemed superficial in comparison with what I was beginning to experience. For the first time in my life, I *possessed* love. I was possessed *by* love.

But I did have a secret that I was too ashamed to discuss, an element of my past that had turned my life into a lie. The secret made me feel that I was someone radically different from whom I had portrayed, and I was always afraid that someone would find out who I really was, where I had really come from.

I found the birth certificate not long after we got broadband. Until then I had mainly used the internet to speak to strangers I met in chat rooms.

The name on the birth certificate was that of a girl I had never heard of, but who shared my first name and birthday. I opened AOL and fidgeted through the pained animal screech of the dial-up. I searched for the name, and it was only then that I realised the girl was me. That was how I found out I was adopted. I was thirteen and I had no idea. I scrolled through the search results, terrified of being caught but unable to stop, feeling entitled to these words that were rightly mine. That was how my adoptive mother found me – hours later – dry-eyed and stoic, squinting at the screen and trying to make sense of it all. She didn't say anything, she just pulled a dining chair up next to me and sat down. For a long time, we sat there not speaking, the silence punctuated only by the clicking and whirring of the mouse. She didn't try to explain or censor, but she sat so close that the warmth of her body held me together like glue as I tried to make sense of what I was seeing. After a while, I asked.

'Did they do it?'

'No,' she said, 'there was no evidence.'

I wasn't sure if that made their abandoning me better or worse.

I was adopted almost immediately after my birth parents were taken away. I was only between families for a few weeks, and I don't remember where I was or what happened to me during that time. I can only imagine that it was neither bad nor good. It never seemed of any importance anyway.

I always felt guilty when I heard people talking about foster families and care homes. I knew that awful things happened to children who were not adequately protected, but I couldn't empathise as I felt I should. People always said that it was the unlucky children who slipped through the net, but I think it was probably the lucky ones – of whom I considered myself an example – who were the edge cases.

After I found out I was adopted, I started to imagine that I could remember fragments of my past life. Certain smells would visit me as I lay in bed at night: lemon furniture polish, stale milk, the synthetic sweet perfume of young women, the stiff cotton of older, sterner ones.

My parents had run a day-care centre, and I imagined that I could remember the faces of the women who worked there, gummy-lashed college students and thick-lined matrons. I had never suspected that I had not always lived with these parents in this house; but when I saw photos of the day-care centre, I wondered if I could dimly recall being there. I had spent the first three years of my life there. Surely it must hold some memory for me. But it just looked normal, nondescript. How anyone believed that such horrors had taken place there surprised me at first, but I suppose that's always the way.

After that day, I spent hours looking at my birth parents' case, trying to conjure memories that might belong only to me. Perhaps I was the only one who could truly know what had happened. It felt traitorous to have forgotten.

◆

I was an only child, but I imagined that I could never have been *the* only child. I feel that I was never put first, but in truth I can't remember. Perhaps this is something I tell myself to justify what my birth parents did, after. When I started school, I was quick to draw comparisons between myself and my peers: there were children who were prettier than me, children who could spell more words, children who made everyone laugh, children who were loving, children who were lovably independent. All these children were better than me. As I grew up, I realised there were people everywhere who were better than me in some way, but I have never seemed alone in feeling like that, in spite of my unique circumstances.

◆

When I googled the name on the birth certificate, I asked my mother if I had been abused. She said I hadn't, and I asked how she could be so sure. I don't remember medical exams. I don't remember police interviews, although sometimes I try to imagine the pressure of the questions they could have asked, the desperate desire to give the right answers. When I was eight, I lied to the optician so I could get glasses I didn't need. I didn't remember it, but it had become a family in-joke, so I knew all about it. How many other lies could I have told, how many secrets could I have kept more successfully, what consequences could there have been for my dishonesty?

Later, I would stare at the pictures of my birth parents I'd found online and try to remember anything I could about them. It was difficult to remove them from the context of the articles I'd read.

'They loved you,' my mother told me that day at the computer, 'and you loved them too.'

I felt sick.

'I don't remember them,' I told her. She smiled that sad smile of acknowledgement and didn't say anything.

There were pictures of police officers escorting them from the day-care centre. The photos were sombre and serene, and I have no reason to believe that they didn't go willingly, with quiet dignity. I can still see those photographs when I close my eyes, and I wonder: why didn't they fight? Do the innocent accept blame so readily?

In the photographs, you could see children's faces in the windows. They were blurred, but I spent hours staring at them, trying to identify which of those children was me. Which of those smudged little faces seemed most confused, most desperate?

Although, I suppose, my birth parents were parents to all of those children in some small way, which is precisely why what they had apparently done was so disgusting.

The pictures I looked at most were those of my birth parents' faces: mugshots, court photos, photos of our family life that the press had dug out. It was more worrying in those days, before family photos could readily be found online.

Their faces were never blurred, and I suppose it's not surprising that they weren't able to continue after all that happened. There was a lot of press coverage, so everyone knew what they had been accused of. In light of the horrible crimes they had allegedly committed, there would no doubt have been a lot of people who were unable to wholly accept their acquittal as truth.

When I looked at the photos, I would ask myself, *Do I look like them?* Was I really made up of those two people? What if they had done what they were accused of? Did that mean I was somehow guilty too? What if they had done it to me? What if I had known about it all, and had blanked it out, and what if the memory came back to me suddenly one day, how would I cope? Or worse, what if it was true, what the papers were saying about me? What if I was possessed, cursed, or worse?

My real memories – the ones that I am sure belong to me – all take place in the world of the parents I know now. I spent hours searching for those lost years but there was nothing there. I asked Georgina, my counsellor, about recovering them once, but she said that it was not worth it, that therapies claiming to recover lost memories were unreliable. I have always wondered if she knew something I didn't, if she was trying to protect me from something.

Sometimes, I try to imagine the children I would have shared my earliest years with, but every time I think I'm getting close, the images become blurry and uncertain. I try to think of what their names could have been, but they blend together: Michelle, Michael, Michaela, Johnson, Thompson, Stone. I can't remember any of them. Sometimes I wondered if I had met some of them, later, in university perhaps, when my name had been changed, and I had been moved to another city. I would always find out where the people I met had grown up, and if they had grown up anywhere near the town where the day-care centre was, I would stay away from them.

I spent a year with my new adoptive parents before I began preschool. It was sort of like an intensive parent–child relationship course that aimed to cover three years of attachment in just one. Having spent all my time until then at the day-care centre, I was intellectually adequate for my age, and I suspect that the year away from other children was to let the dust settle, rather than for my emotional or educational well-being.

My life had been fairly normal since I was adopted. I had no memory of what had happened. When I found out about my past, it was all I could think about. But it seemed abstract, as if it had happened to someone else.

◆

People are always afraid, and if there is nothing to fear, they find something. The fear of any one individual is silly and shameful – no one cares if you are afraid of the dark – but a shared fear, a national fear, is binding, a cause against which we can all unite. Sometimes these fears trigger wars, but more often they form the beginning of something much subtler, something that rises up through the mainstream until it becomes so entrenched in our society that its object can only become real. And when we look everywhere for threats to our normal existence, we inevitably find them.

I never knew the children who made the accusations; their names were never released publicly. It seems likely now that they were simply trying to please when they said they saw my birth parents fly, when they said they were threatened with twelve-inch blades, that they saw babies slaughtered and human blood slurped down like vast, red milkshakes. It seems ludicrous now that anyone listened, but what else can we do for a child in pain except believe them? It was the early 1990s, in the wake of several high-profile cases of so-called Satanic Ritual Abuse in childcare settings around the world. 'Believe the Children' had become a mantra for many who wanted to protect children from unthinkable abuse. It was a few years until anyone would suggest – loudly enough to be heard, at least – that the methods that had been used to interview those children had been suggestive, that the families of those initial accusers had been vulnerable, that media outrage around a heightened fear of cults, violent video games and an onslaught of pop psychology had produced a moral panic on which we could blame all the wrongs in the world. For did it not make more sense for the people who abused children to be possessed by sheer evil? Was it not comforting, in some way, to find a reason for the intolerable; an enemy we could fight with love and purity and God, not guns and nuclear weapons?

When I asked my mum that day if they did it, I wasn't sure which part I was asking about. When she said no, she meant that, in the end, there had been no evidence that any of the children had been abused or neglected, and certainly no evidence of satanic rituals. It was not reported that the majority of the children I spent those early years with had sent loving letters of support to my birth parents, how the accusers withdrew their accusations, how the most vocal parents faded quickly from the public eye. But by the time the panic had died down, it was too late. My birth mother – her name was Amanda – overdosed on sleeping pills shortly after she was released. In the photos of her, I can see my own thin lips and blotchy freckles. My birth father, Ellis, from whom I seemed to have inherited my mousy hair and straight nose, changed his name and disappeared. He needed no reminders of this tragedy. He could not bear to look at me. I never heard from him again.

It was a tragedy; this is how I tried to think of it. My family were victims of a media frenzy. The tabloids had said I was cursed, that I should be exorcised, that I was a carrier of evil. Of course, it was ridiculous, but I couldn't help but be nervous of the occult after I found out. I couldn't stop myself from wondering sometimes if there was any truth to it. If they weren't guilty, why did they never come back for me? Was there some evil in me just waiting to come out?

I never told Owen any of this, because I didn't want him to think I was crazier than I already was.

SEVEN

I scrolled through the numbers in my phone, wondering who I could turn to. Elliott had messaged me asking if Owen was okay and I replied that he was, that he had gone to visit family. It was the only answer I could think of that would prevent him from coming to the flat. There must have been clients expecting to hear from him, and soon there would be bills to pay, but I didn't know the password for his laptop so I couldn't check.

I regretted not getting the password from him, but I had always felt so guilty whenever I accidentally spied on him, reading his messages over his shoulder, or asking for too many details from a night out. I wanted him to share everything with me, but I didn't want him to feel that I was invading his privacy. That was before I consumed him. Now his privacy was the least of my concerns.

More than two weeks had passed, and I had not spoken to anyone about what had happened. Every time I thought about asking for help, or even just talking about my feelings, I was struck dumb. Who would believe me? But it was becoming clear that my coping methods – keeping my head down at work, avoiding my friends, and passing my evenings and weekends in a sweaty, broken half-sleep – were unsustainable.

I had never really thought to expand my social circle outside of Owen, and I felt now that I could only try to talk to someone who did not know him in his own right. I would not be able to explain the events I believed to have taken place, but if I skirted around the issue, I might be able to take steps towards some sort of resolution.

I understood that most people would turn to their families in difficult times, but I had never been that type of person. I had never blamed my parents for not telling me about the adoption. They had done what they thought was right, and it probably did buy us some time to bond as a family. I was grateful to them for taking me on, but it was this active gratitude that I had grown to resent. To be grateful for something meant you had to understand the weight of losing it. This responsibility was too much to bear.

The rift between me and my adoptive parents had opened up during my adolescence; either that, or it had always been there, and I had not realised my own otherness until I was accidentally exposed to it.

As I pondered what was happening to me, I began to realise that – although I had always thought I was close with the person I knew as my mother – I had taken every opportunity to isolate myself from her. My first three periods had been absorbed by wads of toilet paper wrapped around my gusset. It was months until I confided in my mother the secret of this blood that symbolised the separation of myself from her. When I got my first boyfriend, I did not talk to my mother about him. I accepted our relationship – and his insistence that I was doing it wrong – as the natural way of things. I didn't once turn to my mother for advice on how to be a woman, and when she proffered it, I tightened my shell to keep her out. When I first left for university she would check in almost daily, but somewhere along the line she had convinced herself that her love was a burden on me, and had drifted into the background of my life, where I held her at arm's length.

My father and I had never been particularly close, but I had always understood this to be only natural for the relationship between father and daughter, a distance that grows wider as a young woman's sex takes hold. Was it really me who had pushed him away, afraid that letting one man close would somehow spoil me for another?

Perhaps it was this pushing away of my parents that had me pulling Owen into me. I had been failed by two sets of guardians; four bearers of unrequited love that had been withheld or ignored. I had grown starved of love and completely ignorant of it.

For Owen, family was especially important. His mother had evidently not provided him with the support he needed, but his aunt had. He had always told me that I should let my parents get closer to me, but it wasn't until now, having absorbed him, that I felt I could really start to understand what he was getting at.

I know it can't have been easy for my adoptive parents. I always assumed my past had dirtied me for them, that they were suspicious, as if I might someday sprout wings and hooves and call the dark lord into our lives. I regret not asking them how it felt. I had projected my paranoia onto the people who had made it their lives' work to love me, and in doing so I had peeled away a protective layer which I now desperately needed.

With Owen inside me, I was coming to understand a lot about the way I had approached the relationships in my life. But it wasn't just understanding; I was *feeling* things differently. It wasn't like my opinions changed dramatically, or my memories became warped, but I was now beginning to see everything from this perspective that I had always thought was right. I was starting to see the world in the way I thought Owen had seen it, the way I thought it was supposed to be seen.

I scrolled and clicked on the number marked 'home', a label that had never really applied, but had always seemed to be the only option.

'Sweetheart!' My father had the kind of voice a walrus might have if it could speak, booming and gentle. 'We've been meaning to—'

'Ali!' My mother grabbed the receiver, and I could hear her tell Dad to go and pick up the phone in the bedroom, so we could 'have a three-way', which made my toes curl. I waited until I heard the scraping sounds of Dad picking up the bedroom phone, and then I told them that Owen had broken up with me. I wasn't sure how I could have said anything different. But the sentiment was the same: *Something bad has happened, I don't think you can help, but I need you.*

The soft rap of plastic on wood told me my father had put the phone down. He hadn't hung up, just rested the receiver on my mother's dressing table. And then I heard him whisper, 'Have you told her yet?'

'Told me what?' I interrupted.

I was sure they were about to drop the big reveal, to tell me that I was cursed, or possessed. Had they always known this would happen? That at the age of twenty-nine I would consume another human? Within one second, I decided they had figured it all out and were going to put an end to it.

It turned out they had booked a trip to Thailand. They would be gone for ten weeks and were leaving in two days. They told me they had only just booked the tickets, but I didn't believe them. I said I was happy for them.

'Are you sure, sweetheart?' Dad piped up. 'If you need us to be here, of course, we will be?' He ended on a question mark, but I knew that the question was not for me. Of course, I wanted them to stay. An obscene horror had happened to me, and I wanted to rely on my parents to fix it. They were the only people who knew everything I had been through, who probably knew more about my past than I did. I had not expected them to abandon me like this.

I couldn't tell them what had really happened with Owen. They would blame it on post-traumatic stress as a result of my birth parents' arrest, and I did not want them to send me back to counselling, not even with Georgina, who had helped me to accept so much as a teenager. It had been years since I had found out the truth and I had been coping with it marvellously, I thought. Until now.

'Dad, I'll be fine,' I said. 'I don't even know what's going to happen with Owen, and anyway, I've got loads of friends, I'll barely even have time to think about it.'

'That's the spirit!' said Mum. 'And it's all just experience isn't it, for the book? How is the writing anyway?' I held back a scream.

I don't know what I expected them to do. I suppose I thought that seeing as they had tried to rescue me once, they might be able to try again. It seemed a little harsh, going away for nearly three months when I had just been dumped by my partner of a decade. But this was their time, their reward for saving me once. And anyway, they'd already booked it.

I hung up the phone feeling that a lifeline – perhaps my only one – had been pulled away from me. My parents would not be around during the critical point in this crisis. In ten weeks, I thought, the situation would either be resolved, or I would have resigned myself to it. The thought of suffering for longer than that was unbearable.

EIGHT

I carried on going to work. I wasn't ready to quit. Darren kept checking in with me, asking if I was okay – it must have been obvious that I wasn't – so I said I'd been having trouble sleeping. He tried to fold his face into a sympathetic smile, the skin around his mouth puckering as he pursed his lips. I could see he had chosen to believe me, but I could tell it was a choice he had consciously decided to make. I couldn't tell him the truth, that I had absorbed my boyfriend, and in doing so, had realised I deserved more in life. I looked away from him to indicate that I did not want to talk.

I wanted desperately to look again at everything I had seen about my past online. I had read some of the articles so many times that I had memorised them, word for word, but still I wanted to scour them for clues. Was my past the reason for what happened with Owen? Since I suspected that Darren had seen the notes I kept in the drafts of my work email, I had suppressed my desire to scour my past at work; but since the absorbing, it had become an obsession. Afraid that I could be tracked on the office network, I snuck into the bathroom multiple times a day to google myself. I would lean back against the cold tiled wall, slide down onto the floor, unlock my phone, and pick up from where I had left off.

One tabloid newspaper had run a whole campaign calling for my institutionalisation. They had not printed my name, or where I was to be found exactly, but the day-care centre had been named and photos posted in all the national papers. If my birth parents were capable of what they were accused of, the paper said, then surely I was a threat to the children of my town. Wasn't it possible, likely even, that I had been groomed to grow up to do the same, or worse? Who knew what they had done to me? Of course, I understood that this was what tabloids did, and for the most part I had been adept at brushing it off. But now I was starting to wonder if they had been right. A normal woman does not absorb her boyfriend.

I had started coming into the office early in an attempt to surround myself with a normality that was lacking in the flat. I often arrived before Jean, and when I did she was disappointed that I was already there. I felt bad for not saying anything to Darren when he'd offered me a job that should rightfully have been hers. Jean was always early, and always the last to leave. She gave everything to her work in the hope that she would be recognised. She didn't know that her career at the council had stagnated, could not imagine that Darren would not reward her hard work with a promotion. I had tried to be like Jean when I first started at the council – putting in the hours to show my commitment – but I quickly realised that it was thankless. Even if I did want to make a go of this career, I don't think I could have committed myself as fully as Jean did. But I hadn't really wanted it. I had taken the job so that I could say I did something valuable, but really, I had other goals that I thought were more worthwhile. Jean would never have never been so conceited; she worked hard and continued to hope that she would be rewarded for it. I had always thought that was pathetic, but wasn't it even more pathetic to give up hope, set unattainable goals for yourself and carry on regardless, wallowing in self-pity?

One morning, three weeks into sharing my body with my boyfriend, I found myself confronting Jean in a way I had never expected I would. The office had started to fill up around me and I didn't like the feeling of being hemmed in by my colleagues. I pocketed my phone and went into the bathroom. I pulled down my trousers and pants and didn't get up from the toilet seat after I was done. I just sat there, searching for my birth father on my phone. I had used press photos of him for reverse image searches in the past, and over the years I had memorised the names of dozens of men who looked like him. I tried not to look at these men too often, but recently I had been doing it more and more.

My birth father was still out there, probably, and I wondered what he was like now. Did he have a new family, or did he keep to himself? Did he have an accomplished career, or did he do whatever it took to get by? Did he go to church, was he a devil-worshipper, was he an atheist, was he in a cult? Did he ever think about me?

I thumbed through the search results, looking at social media profiles of men who looked like him. Paul Lansman was a menswear designer in Chicago. Chuck Sandberg lived in Ohio and seemed to have three teenage daughters, all of whom looked nothing like me. Steve Smollett was a carpenter in Auckland. Horst Becker was a German politician. They all shared my birth father's chin or his eyes or his haircut. Any of them could have been him and I would never know.

'Allison, is that you?' I dropped my phone at the sound of Jean's voice. She was standing right outside the cubicle. I could see her loafers. I left my phone where it lay on the floor and stayed quiet.

'Allison?'

I sighed.

'Yeah?' I said.

'You've been in here a while, are you okay?'

'I'm fine, I'll be out in a minute.'

'Do you need me to wait?' asked Jean.

'Please don't,' I said, and Jean left.

I buttoned up my trousers and flushed. I turned on the tap and stared at myself in the mirror. I was pale and blotchy. My shirt had a toothpaste stain on it and my hair was greasy. But there was something else in my appearance that had not been there before. I strained my eyes, trying to see myself in profile. My nose was stronger somehow, although it wasn't visibly broader or straighter or longer. The fold of my lips seemed different. They were more upturned or more downturned; I couldn't tell. There was a look in my eyes, reflected by the mirror, that was the look of a person staring at someone else.

The bathroom door burst open, slamming against the wall, and a woman I vaguely recognised from another department barged into a cubicle. I turned off the tap and left.

There was a cup of tea on my desk. Jean peered up at me from beneath raised eyebrows.

'Thanks,' I said. She nodded and smiled. She clearly wanted to say something, but after looking at me for a few seconds, she shut her mouth and sighed. I was grateful for her rare display of tact.

When I got up to leave at lunch, Jean followed me outside.

'Allison!' she called after me. I didn't stop but she caught me up. 'Allison, are you okay?'

'Yeah, fine,' I said, 'thanks.'

'Are you sure?'

'Yes, I'm fine.'

Jean paused. 'How was your meeting with Darren yesterday?'

'Fine,' I said, as if I thought that saying it over and over again would make her leave me alone.

'You know,' said Jean, 'you can always talk to me, Allison.'

'He offered me a promotion,' I snapped. I hadn't meant to say it, but didn't Jean deserve to know? She didn't say anything. 'I asked why he didn't give it to you and he just said you weren't right for it.' I don't know if I meant to be cruel, or if I was trying to be honest, or if I was just trying to get Jean to leave me alone. I was aware that she was trying to be good to me, but I couldn't accept whatever she was prepared to offer. It was so painful to see her making so much effort when it was all futile.

'Oh, well. That's good,' said Jean, 'good for you. You deserve a break.'

'But you deserve it more,' I said.

'It's not about me, Allison.'

'Okay, right,' I mumbled and walked away.

NINE

Owen and I got our first flat together, just the two of us, a couple of years after we graduated. Owen had just been hired as a designer at an agency that seemed to work exclusively with the sorts of brands our friends fetishised. Later I would try to convince myself that settling into a career too early was more dangerous than not, that my own path had been truer and would result in greater job satisfaction in the long run. But I really believed that getting a job directly related to your degree was the holy grail of graduates everywhere, and that by failing to make use of my media studies degree, I was failing to realise my own potential. It was around this time that I began to accept that I was not without jealousy, although I felt desperately that this was not acceptable within the realms of the personality I believed I should have. I understood that there was no threat to me, not really, not more than there had ever been, but I felt angry with Owen constantly. I felt left behind. During that year I broke up with him too many times to count. I never meant it – I couldn't bear to be without him – and I would bang my head against the wall during the desperate times when he did not come back to me readily. Every time my head collided with the wall, I would feel a little more numb. Afterwards, I would text him and apologise. I would cradle my head in my hands until he came back to me.

Every time I would promise that it would be different, and although it never was, the desperation sort of faded over time; either my histrionics became the norm, or I got less paranoid.

Owen made friends with the people he worked with, which I resented because I was alone in the power tools shop, with only cowboy chippies for company, and I was not making any progress with my writing.

I had always thought of myself as popular because I had plenty of friends in secondary school. It wasn't until I left university, and Owen started to build his own network outside of me, that I realised how alone I was. My only real friend was Natalie, who had been my best friend since college. Owen and I had made friends at university, but most of them had moved away, and the ones that were left were people I considered Owen's friends, rather than mine. Natalie was busy with the internship that I was jealous of and was also making new friends outside of me.

It must have been lunchtime when I first noticed Natalie at college, because she was working through a packed lunch in the courtyard, while everyone else ate fast food they had brought back from town. I was smoking, pretending I didn't hate the taste. Natalie was sitting on a bench directly in my line of sight. I watched her take a pot of yoghurt out of a Tupperware box and peel off the lid, which she discarded rather than licked, as a more confident or less lonely person might. She was already a pitiful sight before the football sailed through the air and collided with her head. Yoghurt spurted across her lap. A boy I knew from secondary school, and disliked intensely, came to retrieve the ball and burst into laughter at the white globs spattered across Natalie's crotch and thighs.

'Hey!' I shouted at the boy, who I had shared almost every class with for the last ten years. I didn't have anything else to follow it up with, but I felt protective of Natalie for some reason. She offered a weak smile and I felt sorry for her. Her hair was limp and greasy, her jeans didn't fit right, her skin was aggravated. She reminded me a bit of Sissy Spacek in *Carrie*. I took to her immediately. We had been close friends ever since. Over the last couple of years, I had started to wonder when she had become better than me – prettier, cleverer, more open – and if I liked her as much in light of it.

◆

Owen started to talk more and more about his new colleagues, and I tried to suppress my jealousy. *You're being irrational*, I told myself. I tried to conceal these feelings from him; I was convinced he would agree I was crazy. I understood that my insecurity was something I needed to fix, something I could not expect another person to accept in me. I didn't *want* to feel this way, and so I accepted that my mind was working incorrectly, that I was damaged. But in spite of my deep-rooted insecurities, I thought I was doing a good job of being 'okay'. I knew I could be snippy at times, that I would become dejected and difficult to be around, but I still made an effort to act normal, to prove that I wasn't broken. I would still go out a few times a month with Natalie and I'd meet up with the friends Owen and I had made at university. Much of what I felt was entirely internalised, and while I was certainly a nightmare to be around, Owen had only seen a fraction of my horrific mind, and knew nothing of my horrific past. I thought that maybe, on the outside, I could be seen as an acceptable girlfriend. But then, the autumn after Owen started at the agency, we had a party in the function room of a pub for his birthday, and I realised that I really wasn't okay.

At first, I felt relieved, silly almost. Owen stayed by my side and introduced me to people individually. The people I spoke to were warm and interesting. When they asked questions, I deflected them with questions of my own. I had learned this technique a long time ago. When I found out the truth about my past, I learned to lie. People rarely asked about my adoption, and fewer still pressed further once I told them I had been adopted at three, that I couldn't really remember anything from before that. There had been occasions – stoned afternoons in my student house, candid conversations with drunk strangers – when people had tried to press further. It was then that I learned that what people really wanted was an opportunity to talk about themselves, to be thrown a rope that would allow them to talk about their own lives in a context they had never before considered. And so, at the party, I played up to people's expectations and relaxed into the learned personality I knew I could use to charm them.

I was standing outside smoking on my own when I met her. I had spent most of the night inside, and relished standing out in the cold, clear night and the forced steadying of my breath as I smoked.

She came out laughing over her shoulder. When she noticed me, she smiled and asked, 'Who are you?' She lit a cigarette.

I decided instantly that I didn't like her, but the evening had been going so well, I had been holding myself together admirably.

I smiled and told the girl my name. 'Owen's girlfriend,' I added. Later I realised she must have known that already.

'That's so funny,' she said, although I didn't see why. 'I'm basically Owen's work wife.' She laughed and extended a warm, slim-fingered hand as if she expected a papal kiss on one of her many rings. I couldn't understand why she would say such a thing. Was she trying to make me jealous or was she just oblivious? I tried to loosen my face into a relaxed smile. She introduced herself – Millie – and I pretended I had never heard of her either, although her name had been lingering in the flat for weeks, like the smell of a dead animal trapped in the walls.

Something I would find, over and over, was that these women of whom I became so jealous all had something in common: I should have liked them. These were always the kind of funny, creative and confident women that I craved to be friends with, that I craved to *be*. They were always the kind of women I wanted badly to respect and appreciate rather than envy. Over and over I would fall at this hurdle, and I would question whether the identity I had tried to carve out for myself was really just a mask I used to make myself seem like the person I felt I was supposed to be.

I went home early the night of that party, without saying goodbye to anyone. I had tried to be rational, to relax, but as soon as I let go, my jealousy cramped, and I sunk further and further away from myself. It was cold when I walked home but my blood was boiling. I pedalled my legs so quickly that I tripped over my feet and fell to the ground in a heap. The anger and frustration bubbled inside me as I pushed myself up and ran home; a five-minute sprint that burned my lungs and left me heaving and spitting into the bathroom sink. I banged my head against the bedroom wall, over and over, not quite hard enough to leave a bruise or cut, until I felt calm, and then I got into bed and cried myself to sleep. I woke up when Owen got home, but I pretended I hadn't. In the morning, I said I felt sick, I had probably drunk too much, and I had not wanted him to feel the burden of me on his birthday. He pulled me close and pressed his lips against my hair, so that his voice was muffled when he said, 'You will never burden me. I'm sorry I wasn't there for you.' I loved him so much when he said things like that, but I could never recall that feeling when I most needed it.

TEN

I texted Natalie:

I just feel so sad.

She replied within minutes:

You're allowed to feel sad.

But for how long?

As long as you need.

I couldn't understand why she thought I wasn't worthy of happiness right now. I wondered why I had messaged her at all.

♦

I was locking up my bike outside the pub when I noticed Cara's blond halo through the window. I thought about unlocking it again and cycling home, but she spotted me and waved. I waved back but Cara had already turned away, and a middle-aged bald man who was sitting at the next table over smiled at me.

Cara was bright and perky and I didn't like her. Her shiny hair and bright complexion felt wholly inappropriate given the circumstances. I couldn't understand why Natalie would bring her.

Cara was relatively new to me. I didn't know where Natalie had met her, but they had grown close quickly. I knew it was childish, but I couldn't help resenting Cara for taking my friend away from me. Natalie called Cara a 'fun friend', which she meant as reassurance that our relationship was much deeper. She didn't seem to pick up on the implication of the statement. She was right, though: I wasn't fun.

Natalie stood up, put her arms around my neck and pulled me close to her. She was taller than me, and her body blocked Cara from view. I nuzzled her neck and smelled her sweet breath – eggy like a cake baking – that had never once disgusted me. For that moment, as I revelled in my friend's warmth, it felt as if she had not outgrown me. Why hadn't I confided in Natalie sooner? I had spent so long trying to repress the parts of myself that I thought were somehow inappropriate. But Natalie had always tried to help me, always tried to cheer me up and make me feel better about myself without directly confronting me about my sadness. I didn't know what to tell her about my current situation, but I was so grateful to her for just being there.

'Oh Al,' she spoke with a sympathy I had been craving, 'how're you holding up?' Her breath was warm in my ear and I hoped she'd never let me go.

I could feel tears crawling behind my eyes, like Owen's fingers were searching for a way out. I swallowed and pulled away from Natalie, who had loosened her grip anyway.

Natalie cooed and soothed and stroked my arm. She told Cara it was her round, and Cara gave me a pitying smile before bouncing off without asking what I wanted. I was grateful to Natalie for creating a space for us.

'What happened?' she asked.

'Why's *she* here?' I said, slinging my head in Cara's direction. Natalie recoiled a little as if the words had physically struck her. She knew I didn't like Cara, but she couldn't understand why. I acted as though it was obvious, but in truth, I couldn't quite pinpoint what it was about her that annoyed me. Cara was a poet, and always seemed to be involved in some creative project or other. She complained about being poor, but I was pretty sure her parents paid her rent. She always seemed so smug. Was this an acceptable reason to dislike someone? She wasn't mean, she must have had *some* talent, and her approach to life was different, more interesting than my own. It seemed reductive to say I was jealous of Cara, but I didn't really have another reason to dislike her.

'I had plans with her, Al, I couldn't just bail. She's nice anyway and you said you need friends around you right now.' I loved the way she called me Al, like a beloved granddad, but right then her casualness felt like an insult.

'She doesn't like me.'

'Al, you haven't even given her a chance.'

'I know,' I relented quickly, giving up my fight. 'I'm sorry,' I said, and as it came out of my mouth, I realised I meant it. I *should* give Cara more of a chance. Owen and I had always joked about how false she seemed, how privileged in her effortless success, but Owen had always had more empathy than me. Did he even join in, or was he just humouring me? Occasionally, he would frown when I insulted Cara, and tell me I should not write her off completely. 'After all,' he would say, 'you're always saying you want more girlfriends.' I usually went quiet for a bit after that.

'So, what happened?' Natalie pressed.

'I just woke up after the party and he was gone,' I said.

'What a dick! I can't believe he'd just—'

'It's not like that,' I whined, 'I mean, I don't think it is. Nat, we were having sex and—'

'I have wine!' Cara announced, plonking a bottle and three glasses down on the table. I was about to say that I didn't really drink white wine when I noticed Natalie looking at me with raised eyebrows like a parent expecting a please or thank you from a child. I thanked Cara. I needed to drink something.

'Al was just talking about what happened with Owen,' Natalie said and they both looked at me, waiting. They had obviously discussed it beforehand.

'Nothing,' I said, 'he's just gone.'

Natalie sized me up with her sad eyes. I could tell that she didn't quite know what to think about the situation, but her main response seemed to be pity. I knew that Natalie's approach was to stay quiet, to create a space in which I could allow myself to open up, but Cara had a different take. She continued to talk, filling the silence, I suppose, in an attempt to distract me from my sadness. She spoke about some guy who'd ghosted her, what a mess she was when her last boyfriend dumped her. It seemed overly dramatic, and I was sort of touched that she would talk about herself in that way just to comfort me. I shook a cigarette out of the packet I had laid on the table and wiggled it around to indicate that I was going outside. Natalie had given up smoking a few years ago, and Cara described herself as a 'social smoker'. As she never came out with me, I had always assumed that her idea of 'socialising' only extended to people from whom she thought she could benefit. The judgement felt harsh now.

It wasn't uncommon for me to take an instant dislike to people, although I had never before given it much consideration. I had thought of myself as one of those people who just didn't like other people, and thought that made me cool and aloof, but once again I was using misery in place of personality. If I was honest, I brushed certain people off because I didn't want them to dislike me first. I could accept Cara not wanting to be my friend, because I had already decided I didn't like her. But if I *did* try to be friendly with her and she snubbed me, I would be left with no choice but to believe that there was something wrong with me. Perhaps with Owen gently nudging my feelings like this, I would be able to become a better friend, and in doing so, more of a person in my own right.

I watched Natalie and Cara through the window. Natalie kept her eyes trained on her glass of wine as she talked, and when she stopped, Cara dropped her shoulders and reached out for Natalie's hand. I thought they must be talking about me. I didn't know how they could be talking about anything else.

I went back inside and tried again to find comfort in friendship. Cara and Natalie had been talking when I opened the door to the pub – Cara's hand still resting on Natalie's – but they stopped as soon as I came back in, as if they had been watching the door and waiting for my return. I knew something was happening, there was a bond between them that I was excluded from. I ought to have noticed that something was wrong. Maybe her face *had* been puffy, her eyes lined in red, her hair a little straggly. Maybe she was visibly distraught, and I had been too wrapped up in my own shit to notice.

'I don't want to make it weird, but have you seen him?' I asked. I had tried not to follow this thread, because I knew where he was. But what would people think if I didn't ask? Natalie and Cara exchanged glances.

'No,' Natalie said, and Cara shook her head. 'We haven't seen much of him since he started working at that place,' Natalie added. 'Have you asked that girl?'

'Helena? No. I thought about it, but no.' I sighed. Natalie and Cara waited for me to say whatever I was obviously considering. 'It's just so strange. It doesn't feel like we've broken up. It's more like he just disappeared.'

'Have you reported him, like, missing?' Natalie asked.

'No. His mum phoned about a week after and I just said that I hadn't seen him, I said I was worried, but she didn't really…' I trailed off. They were both staring at me oddly. I wanted to ask them what was wrong, but I knew what they were thinking. They were thinking that Owen had just up and left. Sure, it was a dick move, but it happens, it was an occupational hazard. I knew they thought he had gone to Helena. I had told them about my suspicions and now they could use those to build a story they could understand. They thought he didn't know how to break the news to his mum, didn't know how to own up to any of this. I couldn't tell them the truth.

There was nothing I could say now they knew how upset I was. These women were enlightened, they were forward-thinking, they made their money exploring new ideas, hunting originality. But to them, I had become just another jilted girlfriend, an understandably irrational ex.

'I could text Elliott?' Cara tried. But if she did that, she would learn that I had told him a different story. She could text every single one of Owen's friends, but it would not help to find him.

'No,' I said, 'it's okay.'

Cara took a huge gulp of wine so that she didn't have to say anything. I downed mine and said I had to go.

'Oh, already?' Cara asked. I said yes, but didn't tell her that it was because I found her pity harrowing.

'I have loads to do,' I told them, 'and I'm going to start looking for a new housemate.' I hadn't expected to say that, hadn't known that was what I was going to do. But if I couldn't tell the truth, I needed to act like this was just another break-up. They relaxed. I had given them what they needed: reassurance that I was not going to be their responsibility for much longer. I stood up, and when Natalie did not stand with me, I stooped to hug her.

'See you later, Allison,' she said. 'Take care.'

'Thanks,' I said quietly, and I knew that I was losing my friend. Perhaps that was the price I needed to pay for the relationship I had always dreamed of.

♦

At home, I washed my face and brushed my teeth, put clean pyjamas on and climbed beneath the sheets. I checked my phone, as usual, before bed. I had an email from Natalie and I read it with one eye closed.

Allison, I know you've been having a hard time lately, but I don't think I can keep this up anymore. We always said we would be honest with each other, but lately I've been trying to hold back. You didn't ask me one thing about my life tonight, did you even notice that? You have every right to be self-absorbed at the moment, but honestly? This isn't a new thing. I know you feel unfulfilled in your life, but can't you even bring yourself to care about your friends? I have been trying to be generous with you but there is so much going on in my life right now that I can't handle taking all your shit on as well. I'm up for a promotion, by the way, and I'm probably not going to get it. I've been dating Michael for six months and you've never even asked me about him. We're breaking up. I don't know what else to say, I don't want this to be the end of our friendship, but it's driving me crazy. Please let's talk. I miss you. I miss us. N x.

I had known Natalie for thirteen years and she had never been angry at me like this before. We had never fought. I thought that was a part of what made our friendship so special. There was never any drama between us, I thought we were better than that.

The worst thing about the email was that I knew she was right about me, and I knew I was not in a position to do anything about it. We had grown apart; or more likely, Natalie had grown, and I had stayed the same. Regardless, we were no longer close. I deleted the email, unable to face Natalie's words, and still knowing that I would restore it tomorrow and read it again. I deserved to feel the full weight of the words, just not yet.

ELEVEN

Natalie's email wasn't the first time I had been called selfish, but I had never before understood how that could be truer of me than of anyone else. It was something Owen would come out with when he was most angry with me, and I would get so upset about it that *he* would end up apologising to *me*. It wasn't that I believed I wasn't selfish; it was more like I thought I *deserved* to be.

I had told Natalie – via text message – that Owen had broken up with me, but I had not seen her in person since a few days before Christmas. I hadn't been spending a lot of time with her, and I probably wouldn't have seen her when I did if it wasn't for the Christmas party at the workspace.

'You can come if you like,' Owen had said.

'Oh, I don't know,' I had responded, trying to understand if his comment had been an invitation or a defence.

'You don't have to,' he said, 'I don't think many people are bringing partners.'

So that decided it.

Owen and I would be spending Christmas with our own families. It had been a few years since we had spent Christmas apart, and I was apprehensive about the time away from him. It felt like so much of our relationship was out of my control, and that by being away from him, he had the upper hand. I thought he'd realise that he didn't miss me, didn't even like me, and that he could only come to that realisation if he spent a few days away from me. He would be at the party one night and the following day we would be going our separate ways. I was frustrated that we would not be spending this final evening before the Christmas break together. The four nights we would be apart were now five. Why did he not think about these things? I tried not to let on that I was annoyed, and arranged to meet Natalie to stave off the feelings of inadequacy and jealousy that Owen's partying triggered in me.

I arrived at the pub first and got myself a drink. I didn't think to buy one for Natalie, or to text and ask what she wanted. It was busy in the pub and I was eager to get a table, to get settled. Natalie arrived a couple of minutes after me, dumped her bag, eyed my drink and went straight to the bar. I remember thinking she seemed a little *off*. I imagined she had just had a tough day at work. I knew her job was demanding, but wasn't that true of all jobs? I had thought it a luxury to work in a job you cared about, and I had written off Natalie's concerns about work because of that.

After a couple of drinks, a few of Natalie's other friends started to trickle into the bar. I had noticed her sending messages, but had been too distracted by my own phone to consider that she might be trying to rally up a group of more interesting people to spend the night with. Now that I thought about it, she might have mentioned the promotion, and didn't she say she was dating someone? I couldn't remember. I had been so busy trying to find a balance between pretending that I wasn't obsessed with Owen's whereabouts and checking up on him constantly, that I had barely listened to a word Natalie had said. Perhaps, if I had not learned to automatically give the right responses as I pretended to listen, Natalie would have noticed that I was distracted. But by that point, I had become adept at pretending, so it made sense that, as far as Natalie was concerned, she had told me her problems and I had listened, even sympathised; but I had never followed up, never asked about her life, never done anything to imply that I cared.

When Cara and some of Natalie's work friends joined us in the pub, I took the opportunity to sink deeper into myself. I looked at my phone a lot and smoked too much as an excuse to get outside, away from everyone. While I had become convinced that nobody liked me, Natalie had flourished socially, and perhaps if I had taken the opportunity, I could have found my place among her group of friends. I could have created the social life I thought I wanted, rather than ignoring what was there for me to take.

I don't think I told Natalie I was leaving that night. I had developed a habit of going outside to smoke and never coming back in. Natalie must have been used it. She didn't text to ask where I was. I probably should have noticed that something was wrong then.

I hadn't realised how one-sided my relationship with Natalie had been. Since New Year's Eve, I had been feeling confident in my right to be selfish, but I had been pushing Natalie away before any of this even started. I'd always wanted to believe she was the most important person to me. Aside from my parents, she was the person I had known the longest, the person who had known the most variations of me. But it was more the *idea* of her being my closest connection that appealed. People were always saying friends were more important than boyfriends, and in theory I agreed. But Owen was my life and I couldn't ignore that.

I told myself that Natalie and I growing apart was just a consequence of growing up. People formed close friendships when they were children or teenagers, but when they grew up, they got careers, had children, moved to new countries. The focus of their lives shifted. Even as I told myself this, I continued to value the idea of myself as friend first and girlfriend second. So, I tried to make an effort with Natalie. I would text her about a new series I was watching, send her long rambling emails at work, try to make sure I saw her every week. When we were together, I took photos and tagged her in them. At least my social media presence made it look like I was a good friend.

But since Owen had started to change, I had become less vigilant over my relationship with Natalie, and looking back, I suppose I started to actively push her away. When she texted me, I was annoyed that the messages weren't from Owen. I stopped asking her to meet up, and when she invited me out, I only accepted if Owen had plans with Helena or the others from the workspace. When I did go out, I would drink fast, eager to be having more fun – getting drunker – than Owen would be.

I had not noticed the difference in our friendship because I had only adjusted the way in which I was using her, whereas she noticed almost immediately. She had not previously been aware that she was being used.

Natalie was my only friend who knew me before I was Owen's girlfriend. There were a few people from our university group who I'd sometimes go out drinking with, but they were tightly wound into my life with Owen, they weren't *mine*. Natalie was the only friend I did not share with Owen, so maybe it made sense that she was the first to give when I felt him slipping away. I had always loved the feeling that being with her gave me. With Natalie, I felt that I understood my place in the world. I felt separate from Owen, that I had a life outside of him, and this validated my existence as a single entity, rather than simply an extension of him. I hadn't meant to let her slip away, but when I started to lose him, I slowed down in my pursuit for independence, my desire to *be something*. I knew that I had been selfish – using my friend in an attempt to create the life I thought I should be living – but I had never considered that it might have been different for Natalie. What did she get out of being my friend? I was someone to go to the pub with, or someone to text when she was bored. Was that the meaning of friendship? If so, wasn't that also self-serving?

I forced myself to restore the email and, as I read it again, I started to cry. What other people thought of me had always been important, but what I had failed to register was that it took very strong feelings for people to tell you what they *really* thought. For so long I had focused on my relationship with Owen, on making him love me with a passion to rival my own, that I had neglected to consider the effect on the people I had pushed to my periphery. It was not just Natalie. I hadn't spoken to any of my uni friends in months; I had all but forgotten they existed. Cara and Elliott and a number of other friends of Natalie's and Owen's had always tried hard with me, and I had always been difficult. I had assumed Owen's friends would talk about me behind my back – Owen's crazy girlfriend – but this in itself was indicative of my self-aggrandising, my belief that I could make no effort with others and still be worthy of their scorn or judgement.

TWELVE

It was four weeks after I absorbed him, after I lost my parents to Thailand and my best friend to my own selfishness, that Owen's things started to move. He had left a book on the bedside table. He had been saying he was reading it for six months, but I hadn't seen him pick it up in at least four. It had just been sitting beside his bed, gathering dust. It was typical Owen. He never seemed to feel like he was *supposed* to be doing something. So, it didn't make any sense when I tripped over the book, one pristine corner poking out from beneath the sofa. Even if he had left it there, which he hadn't, surely I would have noticed it? And then I found his clothes in the washing basket, when I knew I had emptied it hours before. The windows kept opening themselves, and one time a mechanical pencil, that he would often use to sketch in the evenings, rolled out from under the sofa.

Wafts of hot lager breathed into my face in the night; musty sweat mixed with deodorant; the gluey scent of the workspace that clung to his clothes for hours after he came home.

My dreams had been gathering intensity, until it felt like they were burying me alive every time I went to sleep. I could never remember their exact content, but I could recall the feeling of being trapped somewhere wet and thunderous, pink and spongy as a tongue. I had often had anxiety dreams and nightmares from which I would wake up soaked in sweat, damp sheets rapidly cooling around me; but those dreams had been memorable, understandable, normal. Now I was waking up in strange places, like the bathroom floor with my face pressed against the damp bath mat, or in the kitchen with my fingers resting on the dials of the gas cooker. I would wake up calm and gradually the terror would build as I came to understand that I was not in my bed. I would freeze in position, listening for danger before running back to my room and diving under the covers.

The flat became unbearably cold. There was always a window open somewhere. It seemed that whenever I was in the flat, I was rushing around closing windows in one room, only to find others newly opened somewhere else.

I was hesitant to think that Owen was haunting me. The notion of it seemed ridiculous, in spite of what was happening. Accommodating him had been horrifying at first, but I hadn't felt scared exactly. It was odd how quickly I had grown used to it, welcoming the new aspects of my personality that he seemingly spurred. But it was only when the poltergeist activity began that I really became frightened. Absorbing Owen had brought him closer to me but there was something so conventional about the paranormal that terrified me. It didn't fit with the experience as I understood it. Although I had lost him, physically, I had gained so much through absorbing Owen. I could see that it had been a positive experience, but I was becoming anxious, realising that I wouldn't be able to continue like this. And a very small part of me was afraid that I was not the only person this had happened to. That maybe people absorbed their partners all the time. That my love was not unique after all.

I had felt uncomfortable in the flat since I returned on New Year's Day, but the discomfort was turning into real fear. I was afraid that it would not be long until violence blossomed, and I would be found one day, dead at bottom of the stairs, leaving nothing behind but a legacy of clumsiness and a ghost story that no one believed.

While I didn't tell Owen what I knew about my birth parents, or about the day-care centre and what had allegedly happened there, bits and pieces of my past had trickled out over the years. I was never sure why he didn't ask more questions. I had tried to tell myself that it was down to tact, but in my less secure moments, I believed he didn't care.

I had told him that I was adopted, that my parents had taken me in when I was three. I had told him that I didn't remember much from before then, which was true. I wondered how I could tell him what I *did* know. I wouldn't need to say much, I thought, he would be able to look it up for himself. I'd probably encourage that, so that I didn't have to talk about it. I hadn't talked about it for a very long time.

I was beginning to wonder if he hadn't asked because he already knew. I had no idea how he could have found out, but after I absorbed him, I felt much more self-assured; less like a person with a secret, and more like a person with a past that did not define them. Why had I been so ashamed? Wasn't it almost funny, the absurdity of it? It would have made a good story; telling it could have made me a more interesting person.

◆

The sky was the dull shade of an unpolished fork. Christmas decorations still hung from lamp posts, limp as executed witches. Adverts for sales adorned shop windows, promising hope to those who couldn't usually afford it. All that was left was the things nobody wanted.

It was becoming apparent that absorbing Owen could have more damaging effects than I had yet been able to predict. I felt that I was becoming dislodged, as if I could slip into total insanity at any moment.

I moved through the city in a daze, and kept finding myself in places with no recollection of how I got there. I had been moving in the general direction of the workspace, but on a sort of whistle-stop tour of the locations of my own personal failure. At one point, I found myself gawking up at the elaborate facade of the museum where I would sit opposite the smooth, black skeleton of a giant elk, a notebook in my lap, held open by the spine, squeezed between my thighs. I don't remember any of what I wrote in there; I tore out the pages when I got home, ripping them into dozens of tiny pieces so nobody could reconstruct my thoughts. Then I was on a bench in a graveyard filled with bodies for whom nobody grieved. It was the quiet spot where I would simmer; the space that Owen had later found (or that I had led him to), that became the site of our most vicious arguments and reconciliations.

I wished I could talk to Owen, but I didn't know what I would say. I didn't exactly miss him, although I longed for the warmth of his body and the smell of his unwashed hair. His individual spirit within me was already starting to fade. I was feeling less that I was accompanied or occupied by Owen, and more that I was on a path to becoming more content with myself in the way that I had hoped I would as our relationship matured. What had happened seemed less abnormal, and more a part of my natural growth. I was no longer the weak one and he the strong. I was slowly becoming an amalgam of the both of us. I was losing sight of him as an individual, but had I ever really had it?

Drilling sounds squealed from one of the studios, and I prayed that Elliott, or one of Owen's other friends, wouldn't come out and talk to me. I hadn't seen Elliott since the party, and I didn't think I could deal with him. I had seen online that he and Cara had been growing closer. They would have discussed me and Owen, would have shared the conflicting stories I had told them. They would demand to know where he was, and I would not have an acceptable answer for them. Looking at pictures of them together, I felt myself understanding Cara's appeal, and the appeal of women like her. She was confident, of course; she was outgoing, she could carry a conversation, she could make you laugh. She was ambitious and bright and distinctly gorgeous. But she was also vulnerable and had insecurities of her own. The difference between me and her was that Cara's vulnerability was not the essence of her; she was a woman with vulnerabilities, not a vulnerable woman.

I had made a mistake. I didn't want to talk to anyone, especially about Owen. What could I possibly say? I couldn't have picked a worse place to be.

I saw a flash of Helena's chestnut hair, a French braid hanging down her back like a horse's tail or a noose. My breath caught in my throat, and I huffed as hard as I could to shove it down or push it out. I didn't know if I was forcing myself to hyperventilate or if it was something that was just happening to me; I had always struggled to discern the root of my guilt. Cold fingers of sweat stroked my skin. I spun around to get away from

Helena, from Elliott, from the workspace and all it represented as fast as I could. I hit a wall of black felt and fake fur and fell to the ground.

'Allison! Oh my god, are you okay?'

Maggie's laugh was good-natured. She dropped her bags to the floor to help me up. When she caught my eye, her face softened and fell.

'Oh Ali,' she said. 'Come on, I'll put the kettle on.'

I didn't know what else to do, so I followed her.

Once we were inside, I told her that Owen was gone. A sympathetic sigh escaped her, seemingly against her will, as if she had been squeezed in a too-tight hug. She pulled me close, resting her palm on the crown of my head, and then stroking my hair which now clung to my scalp in greasy, matted clumps. I leaned my head into the soft wool of her jumper, and left beads of saliva clinging to the fibres. She pretended not to notice as she pulled away and looked at me.

'You mean you've broken up?' she asked.

'No, I mean he's gone!' I said, my voice strained like a bratty child's. I sounded as dramatic as I had hoped, for the situation warranted it for once, and I needed her to understand. Maggie raised an eyebrow.

'I don't know where he is!' I squawked and started crying. I told her that we had stayed in a hotel on New Year's Eve, which she already knew, and I told her that Owen was not there when I woke, which she did not.

'You didn't see him leave at all?' she asked. I said no. And partly because I thought Maggie seemed the most likely person to have the propensity to understand what had happened, and partly because I could not bear the singular loneliness any longer, I began to fill in the gaps.

'I have this sort of weird memory,' I ventured. 'When we got back from the party, we had sex, and I kind of remember him sort of... disappearing?'

'Disappearing during sex?' Maggie scoffed. 'What a dick!'

'No...' I sighed, struggling for the words to describe it. 'I mean, it was like he just... vaporised, or like I... absorbed him or something.'

Maggie thought about that for a minute.

'And you haven't seen him since?' she asked.

I said no.

'Have you told anyone?' she said.

I replied that I had been telling people that Owen had broken up with me, that it was easier to explain that way, because with break ups people knew when to stop pushing for details. I told her that Owen's mother had called and had sounded angry at him, as if it was something they had discussed, that she had tried to talk him out of. She had only called the once, but that was a month ago, it would only be a matter of time before she called again and what was I supposed to say then? I had become near-hysterical by that point, choking out the words on heaving sobs, thick and sloppy as meat fat.

Maggie sighed and repeated my name back to me several times. There was no fear or confusion in her voice; only kindness, and empathy, as if she understood what I was telling her. She pulled me close again and stroked my hair until my breathing slowed to a manageable pace.

'You must have been so frightened,' she said.

'That's the thing, though,' I choked. 'I wasn't really. It just feels... normal... Well it did, but now things keep moving in the flat... his things and I just... I'm losing it, aren't I?'

I had calmed a little by then, my tone growing more resigned than panicked. I threw the soggy tissue I had been clutching into the bin and dropped my head into my hands. I rubbed my eyes. Maggie rummaged around in her bag and pulled out a rough-cut crystal dangling from a leather cord.

'I know it's not really your thing,' she said, 'but I really think this could help you. At the very least, it'll make me feel better. Will you wear it?'

The necklace was ugly, the kind of nineties throwback that was making its way back into fashion. I knew Maggie was into crystals – I had written them off as another hippy quirk to be ignored – but the jewellery she usually made was much more original than this. I realised I didn't have anything to lose, and I didn't want to upset her, so I nodded and took it. Her eyes were wet and wide. She pulled the cord around my neck, and once she had fastened it, she loosened up.

'Look, why don't you come and stay with us for a few days? Julian's mum bought Seren this godawful tent thing and she's been camping in the den since Christmas. You can stay in her room. You'd be doing us a favour, actually. Sometimes, Jules and I, we forget we're not twelve too. Having an adult around would be great!'

I tried to look like I was thinking about it; I had known Maggie was going to invite me, and I had known what I was going to say. I needed some space away from the flat and its haunting to figure out what I was going to do next.

'Oh Mags, are you sure? I don't want to be any—'

'Oh, shut it, you'll make me cry, I'm all soft these days. Look, I've got a few bits to do here. Jules is picking Seren up at three, they'll be home by the time you've packed a bag. I won't be long.'

Maggie was already hustling me to the door. I hugged her, and she laughed and brushed me off. 'Don't say anything,' she said.

THIR T EEN

I was sitting on a wall near some unoccupied units in the workspace estate when I first met Maggie. Owen had just started working there, and I had tried to visit him, but he was busy. A sound from the recycling bins startled me. My first thought was rats, but then I heard what sounded like a woman grumbling. I stared.

'Gotcha!' said the disembodied voice, and a green recycling sack came flying from the direction of the bins. Maggie tumbled out, picked up the recycling bag, and started to work on the knot.

'Oh,' she said, noticing me. 'Hi there.'

I didn't respond. Maggie cleared her throat and turned her attention back to the knot. After a minute or so, she turned to look at me again, holding something small between her thumb and forefinger.

'It's a commission,' she said, 'I've been working on it for months.'

'Oh,' I said, 'what is it?' I don't know why I asked. I had only wanted to sulk in peace, and now I was actively showing interest in a stranger.

'It's a ring,' she said, walking over to me and holding the ring out. When I made no move to look closer, she took my hand, held it out in front of her, and dropped it into my palm.

'It's pretty,' I said, even though I didn't really think it was.

'Thanks,' she said, 'that's a real emerald, biggest one I've set before, and these are diamonds, from some grandmother's engagement ring.'

'Oh,' I said.

'I make jewellery,' said Maggie.

'Yes,' I said.

Maggie retied the recycling bag and slung it back into the bin. When she was done, I held the ring out for her to take.

'You okay?' she asked, pocketing the ring.

'Yeah,' I said, 'I'm okay.'

'Fancy a coffee?'

'Yeah,' I said, for reasons I could not fathom. I let an awkward laugh slip. 'Yeah, okay.'

I was surprised by my response, but Maggie didn't seem phased. I trusted her immediately. I wanted to be around her – something I hadn't felt about a stranger in a long time – so I followed her to the coffee shop.

Owen was there. I tried to avoid his eye, but when I caught it, I forced myself to wave a sheepish little wave. He waved back and smiled a small, flat smile.

'Who's that?' asked Maggie.

'My boyfriend,' I said.

'What's his name?'

'Owen.'

'And what's your name?'

She was cracking me open, but doing it so gently that I wouldn't notice.

'Allison.'

'Well, hello, Allison. I'm Maggie.'

Maggie asked me questions about myself. I gave short, vague answers, and then she gave me the answer that she would have given if I had asked.

'Do you have any brothers or sisters?'

'No.'

'No, me neither. People always say it must be weird being an only child, but I quite like it. Are you close to your family?'

This is how I found out most of the demographic information I know about Maggie. She was forty-two or forty-three; unbelievably only a year or two younger than Jean. She was married to a tech entrepreneur with whom she had a twelve-year-old daughter. She used to do admin for a company that made herbal teas, but now her husband – Julian – had sold his business and she didn't have to work any more. Julian rented a desk in the workspace, and it was he who had signed Maggie up for a unit for the jewellery business she had been half-heartedly starting up for years. Maggie had grown up in Weston-super-Mare and was glad to be raising her daughter – Seren – in the city, where whatever trouble she got into would not be reminiscent of Maggie's youth on the pier.

'Hey, where did Owen go?' she asked eventually. 'I hope I'm not keeping you!'

I told her I had just finished visiting him when I saw her by the bins. He would have gone back to work.

'It's okay, we live together,' I said. 'I'll see him in a few hours.'

'He seems nice,' Maggie said, even though she had not spoken to him, and for some reason I found myself opening up about our relationship.

It was the first time I had been to the workspace, but Owen had been working there for close to a month by that point. I had called in sick at work, but I felt fine, so I had taken a walk to visit Owen. He was putting on his jacket when I saw him across the room and headed over to his desk.

'What are you doing here?' he'd asked.

'Surprising you!' I said. 'Do you want to go to lunch?'

'I'm sorry, Al, I can't, I have plans.'

'Owen, are you— oh, hello.' I had heard of Helena. Owen had recently started dropping her into conversations, casually, overly cautious in case he communicated a threat. He introduced us, and Helena made as if to hug me, so I thrust my hand out for her to shake.

'I'm going to help Hel with her new website. I'm sorry, I'll see you later though?' Owen said. I was so embarrassed. Why did I think I could just show up and expect him to drop everything for me? He wasn't scolding me or making a scene, but I felt everyone was looking at me, thinking about how desperate I was, what a loser.

'Of course,' I said and forced myself to kiss him on the cheek. I waved at Helena, making an effort to smile on my way out. Then I went to sit on the wall, where Maggie found me.

It wasn't just the nature of the exchange with Owen that had rattled me. I had already decided that Helena must be better than me: more creative, more inspired, more confident, more beautiful. I wasn't consciously angry at him for having lunch with her instead of me, except, in a way, I was. I couldn't reconcile the differences between my rational self and my emotionally heightened one. All I knew was that I was upset, and without the language to express why, I felt more than ever that my normal-person facade was slipping.

Maggie listened without interrupting. She didn't say anything until she was certain I had finished.

'Sounds tough,' she said. 'How do you feel about him working here?'

So I told her about Owen quitting his job, going freelance and renting a desk, all without discussing it with me.

'I didn't want him to ask permission,' I said, unsure if I believed myself, 'but I thought we would have talked about it.'

'Yeah,' said Maggie, 'that is odd. I guess he's just adjusting, though. You're not worried about that Helena, are you?'

'I don't know,' I said. 'I know I shouldn't be, but it's hard not to.'

'Well, I'll keep my eye out,' Maggie offered, 'and you're always welcome to visit *me*! Oh! Is that the time, I really should get that ring in the post.' Maggie downed her coffee and stood up.

'I'm sorry for keeping you,' I said, 'and thanks, for everything.'

'Oh, shush you, we have to do this again.'

'Of course,' I said, already certain that a second meeting would not happen.

'How about Friday lunchtime? Meet you here at one?'

'Oh, yeah, okay.'

'Great. Okay, I really need to go. I'll get your number next time, so just promise you'll be here Friday?'

'I promise,' I said.

She hugged me and then she was gone.

◆

Since Owen had gone freelance, I had become more and more erratic and irritable. It made no sense that I would have made a friend in that time. But I was so grateful to Maggie, who had responded to my broken story with the empathy and grace I wanted so badly to be able to offer others. I had explained myself poorly, had shared only crazed snippets of an unbelievable story, and yet Maggie had not responded with questions and answers, as most friends would, but with quiet acceptance that made me feel more stable than I had in months.

◆

When I got back to the flat, Owen's best trainers were back in their rightful place in the row by the front door. I couldn't remember if I had put them there. Had I unpacked his bag? What I was sure of was that I had made the bed before I had gone out. I had forced myself to look back into the bedroom and memorise what I had seen, to create a frame of reference for my own instability. But when I looked at the bed, I saw that the sheets were pushed back at one corner, as if someone had just got out and was expecting to get back in again. I smoothed the sheets with my fingers. I had expected them to be warm, but they weren't. Somehow, this was more unsettling.

I leaned back against the headboard and set my laptop on the duvet in front of me. I opened Natalie's email and hit reply.

You're not wrong about me. I am selfish. I always have been. I'm sorry. There's a lot you don't know about me, and you don't know because I have kept secrets from you. I was supposed to be your best friend. I was bad at it. The truth is that my birth parents might have been Satanists. And they might have put a spell or a curse on me. Owen didn't leave me. I absorbed him. I don't know if he's alive or dead. All I know is that he's inside me.

There was no way I could send that. I deleted what I had written and started again.

I'm sorry Natalie.

I hit send.

FOURTEEN

Owen had never been sure whether he wanted children or not, but I had. People were always saying that you changed when you had children of your own. They would say this like it was a good thing, but it was precisely that change that I was afraid of. I laughed it off when people asked – as they had increasingly begun doing in recent years – saying, *Why would I have children when I could have dogs?* And, *There's just no way I'd give up going to the pub for that!* I joked that if I had children, I would shake them or hit them or just neglect them entirely. I would feel the atmosphere flex when I said that. Most people I spoke to were aware that I had been adopted, but no one knew why. Sometimes it can be difficult to tell the difference between jokes and complete honesty around deep-rooted fears. I suppose my friends thought I was trying to tell them something. I let them take meaning where they thought they found it; the worse they thought my childhood had been, the less likely they were to ask questions.

The worst thing about being expected to have children was being told how much more fulfilling life would become once you had given birth, as if my role in life was moot unless I had a child. People thought that for women, pushing your body to its maximum capability was the only way to find true fulfilment. Did they not know that over eight hundred women died from pregnancy-related complications every day? That millions of women were not capable of giving birth? Did these women not deserve fulfilment, were they disqualified from it?

If not having children meant that I would never be happy, why shouldn't I just end it all there and then? I tried this argument once or twice before I retired it; I did not want to become known as a suicide risk. Eventually, I learned to say that I knew I might change my mind someday. I didn't really believe it, but I said it because I could not bear the smug pity of a person telling me about their friend – *she was just like you* – who now had three children and was happier than ever. Or worse, that flash of darkness in the eyes of a person when they saw the entire lack of the maternal in me, as if I was void of anything even resembling humanity.

◆

I'd been to Maggie's house for dinner a couple of times before, and I'd met Seren both at their home and at Maggie's studio. I didn't much like her at first. I didn't know how to talk to children. Later, Maggie told me that Seren was a 'huge Allison fan', but I didn't believe her. After that, I tried to stay out of her way.

'Hey, Ser,' I said, when she answered the door. I regretted instantly the overfamiliar tone I found myself putting on. I thought I saw her flinch.

'Hi, Allison. Dad's just on the phone but he said to just come in and make yourself at home.' She pulled the door wider so that I could step through. 'Are you staying for dinner?'

'Yeah,' I said, 'I might actually stay for the night too.'

'What's wrong with your place?'

I finished pulling my shoes off and stood up straight.

'Oh, nothing really,' I said, 'I just fancied some company.'

'Dad says Owen left you.'

'Oh. Well we broke up, I guess.'

'Do you miss him?' Seren asked, and while it hurt me to be asked questions like this, it also made me warm to her. She had no reason to expect that this level of candidness would affect our relationship. Love, for her, had always been unconditional.

'Yes and no,' I said, because I felt she deserved my honesty. 'I guess I'd rather not talk about it.'

'Got it,' said Seren, and she pulled me by my arm into the living room where she was watching old episodes of *Friends*.

Maggie came home after two episodes, rustling with bags and jingling with jewellery. Seren didn't look up when she came into the living room, and Maggie just ruffled her hair and said, 'How's it going, girls?'

'Fine,' said Seren.

'Maggie, thank you so much for—' I began.

'Nope!' said Maggie. 'If you want to thank me, come and help me make dinner.'

I sliced vegetables and grated vegan parmesan as Maggie fussed around me.

'I've been thinking about it,' she said, 'and I hope you don't mind me being so blunt but, well, is something... *truly supernatural* happening, do you think, or do you think he's just gone?'

I thought about it for a minute. I couldn't bear to change my story now. If Maggie couldn't believe it, no one would be able to, but at least Maggie wouldn't think of having me sectioned. 'I don't know,' I said, honestly. 'The way I remember it, I absorbed him, physically, while we were—'

'And now he's… haunting you?'

'No. I don't know. Maybe?'

Maggie frowned a little, more in concentration than confusion. 'What are you going to do?'

'I don't know.'

'Ladies!' Julian announced as he sauntered into the kitchen, first kissing Maggie on the cheek, and then me. Julian was a loud man, full of confidence and warmth, only occasionally intimidating. He had started up his own business many years ago and had just sold it for a figure he never spoke of, but that I had read about online. He was currently starting up a new tech business, some app to help creatives and freelancers manage their workload or something. He had a desk at the workspace which he frequented rarely. He might have noticed Owen's absence, but he knew better than to ask anything, trusted Maggie to take care of it. He was the kind of man I could imagine Owen growing into, the kind of man I wanted to love one day, but not yet.

At dinner, I asked Seren what she wanted to do when she grew up. Maggie gave me a sly smile that told me I was going to regret asking. Seren started by saying she thought it was cool that I worked at the council. I wondered if Maggie had made her say that, but even as I did, I felt warm and proud, something I had not felt in as long as I could remember. Seren said she couldn't bear it that so many people didn't have homes, and she thought more people should be helping them. She wanted to be a vet herself, or maybe an actress, but if she was an actress, she would donate at least half of what she earned to animal charities and she'd insist on having important roles that made people think about being better. She had thought about being a singer, she said, but she didn't think it was realistic and the music industry seemed pretty brutal. She was going to carry on singing, though, because the best actresses were multitalented and besides, she liked it. It was difficult to keep up with her ambitions, but I tried my best to give the requisite responses.

After dinner, Julian went to his office in the attic and Maggie, Seren and I went into the living room. Maggie picked up an art book and dropped into an armchair and Seren sat next to me on the sofa. I don't remember what we watched, or for how long. The fact I can't remember those hours makes me think I must have slipped away from it all, and perhaps those were the happiest hours I'd had in some years.

Eventually, Maggie slapped her knees and said, 'Right then,' and Seren jumped up and ran upstairs.

'I hope Ser's room's okay for you,' said Maggie, 'she tidied it this morning, but god knows what it's like now.' I tried to smile and say that I was really grateful, but I'm not sure if that's what I did. Seren bounded down the stairs clutching her pyjamas, an iPad and a little diary with a padlock on it. She went into the den, where a kid's play tent was set up.

'Cool tent,' I said as I passed her.

'Uh, thanks,' she said, 'it's kind of babyish but we want you to be comfortable.'

It makes me uncomfortable when kids try to act grown up.

There were posters in Seren's room of people I thought I recognised. A menagerie of stuffed animals had evidently been relocated recently to underneath the bed and the head of a fluffy giraffe poked out. Spots of Blu-Tack on the wall suggested a recently taken-down poster, and I wondered what Seren was so ashamed of.

I was scared of Seren because I had been so solid in my belief that I was in no way maternal. I had seen her in the role of *daughter*, and this had frightened me. I was starting to understand that the world wasn't so black and white. Perhaps I could be a kind of role model for Seren. Not wanting children of my own didn't mean I had to avoid children altogether. I wondered if this was why Owen had been undecided about whether or not he wanted to be a parent. Perhaps I could provide something motherly to the people I loved by being more open and accepting of them. Maybe not wanting to be a mother didn't mean I was lacking something.

Being with Maggie, Julian and Seren had also got me thinking about my own family. We had been close when I was Seren's age. I had not yet found out that I was adopted, and my adolescence had not yet cracked the solidity of our family unit. Not knowing what had really happened with my birth parents affected my relationship with my adoptive parents. I learned that caretakers could be capable of anything. How could I be expected to trust anyone? I regretted pushing my parents away. I googled the time difference and, satisfied that they'd be awake soon, if not already, I called my mum. She answered on the second ring.

'Allison, darling, how are you?' She sounded sleepy.

'Did I wake you?' I asked.

'Oh no, your dad and me just got up to watch the sunrise on the beach. We've done it every morning since we've been here. It's beautiful, wait a second.' I heard her tapping on the phone screen, whispering to my father. 'Oh, I can't figure out how to take a photo while I'm on the phone, do you know?'

'I'm not sure,' I said, even though I was. I understood that admitting my technical competence to my parents would result in a lot of questions I was too impatient to answer.

'Never mind, I'll take one tomorrow. How are you? It must be late there?'

'Yeah, it's pretty late. I'm staying at Maggie's. I just didn't feel like being alone.'

'Oh, Allison, I hate to think of you so sad. I wish there was something we could do. Do you want us to come home?'

'Don't be silly, Mum,' I said. Tears were streaming from my eyes, but I tried to hold my voice steady. I wished she would come home and hold me. If she were there, I would probably tell her everything, even if I did think she'd just get me locked up. Maybe that was what I needed. She would have known what to do.

'We can come back, you know, if you—'

I hung up. I squeezed my eyes shut and took three deep breaths. When I opened my eyes again, my mum was calling. I answered.

'Sorry about that,' she said, 'I don't know what happened. What was I saying?'

I swallowed the lump in my throat.

'Just what a good time you're having,' I said.

'Oh, yes. Are you sure you're okay, Allison?'

'Yeah,' I said, 'I'm okay.' I paused. 'I love you, Mum.'

'I love you too, darling,' she said.

'Love you three!' I heard my dad shout.

'I'd better go to sleep,' I said. 'Goodnight, Mum.'

Lying in Seren's single bed, I watched the silhouette of an enormous house spider creeping on the outside of the pale pink princess canopy. I could still feel Owen's presence spooking around inside me. It didn't matter where I was, if I was alone or not. This was my life now, and I needed to take control of it.

♦

In the morning, Maggie brought me a cup of tea in bed. Her cat bought me a mouse and I threw it out the window onto the street, which I would regret when I passed it on my way out later. Maggie sat on the edge of the bed and I, still under the duvet, sat up against the headboard. For the first time, I thought Maggie looked old, like a mother. Her interest in my wellbeing seemed somehow less special in that context, like she was in some way obliged to care, forced into sympathy against her will.

'I think I'm going to go home tonight,' I said.

Maggie said, 'Oh,' and then she smiled and said, 'of course, but you're welcome here anytime, you know? I mean it.'

I was grateful, but when I thanked Maggie it came out dry, sarcastic, so I tried to sound positive instead.

'I'm going to need to get a room-mate; there's no use hanging around, is there?' I offered a smile as weak as Maggie's tea and she smiled back, pity glinting in her eyes like broken glass. Part of me wanted to ask her what to do, but the rest of me didn't want to hear her take on things. I was not her responsibility.

Julian and Seren had already left when I came downstairs. Maggie was in the shower. I made a piece of toast and ate it dry. The cat was snaking around the garden when I left the house without saying goodbye. I kicked the mouse in the cat's direction. The cat pounced and then wandered off nonchalantly when it realised the mouse was already dead.

FIFTEEN

I started in the office. I don't know why we called it that. It was a spare room and we only used it for storing junk. I suppose when we first moved in, we thought we would use the extra space productively.

'You can write in there,' Owen had said.

'Why can't I be with you?' I'd whined, half-joking.

Owen laughed, not quite sure what to do with my insecurity. Whenever I became overwhelmed by work or the general lack of ambition in my life, he would suggest I go into therapy. He didn't know that I had spent many of my teenage years working through my own origin story with a counsellor. He didn't know I had any reason to. I was never sure if he was writing off my anxieties as trivial, or actually trying to help me. He'd lost his temper with me a handful of times, and he'd tried to break up with me once or twice.

'I just don't think I can give you the support you need,' he had said. 'I can't cope with it any more.' I understood what he was saying – I was crazy – so I stopped talking to him about it and kept my fears to myself.

The less I spoke openly about my fears, the more they accumulated. Trying to hide my insecurities from Owen meant I needed to spend a lot of time internally, and in doing so, I found myself making space for the other concerns I had tried to block out. What if I had been abused as a child, and everybody had thought it better that I didn't know? How would I be different if that were true, if I knew about it and had worked through it? What if my birth parents really *were* Satanists, performing rituals on innocent children, using my body as a host for evil? It explained everything that was wrong with me. As the fears snowballed inside me, I became more selfish, more unbearable. The more I worried, the more Owen's love seemed like a struggle. Had I opened up to him, he might have been able to accept me as I was. I had thought that he didn't want me to open up, that he wasn't interested in who I was. Now I was beginning to think that I had been wrong. If he had been afraid of my honesty, I would feel it now, as part of my own anxiety and shame. But all I felt was a creeping self-acceptance. I had been wrong about what he felt for me. I could feel the dregs of his compassion and love.

◆

Most of the stuff in the spare room was junk, and I didn't find it difficult to throw it away. I never understood how people got addicted to cleaning, but perhaps what they really got addicted to was escaping the mess of their everyday lives.

I found the box of papers at the back of the built-in wardrobe that we initially used for coats, but which had quickly filled up with clothes we had hoped we would be able to fit into again one day (mine) and that we had meant to repair at some point (his). The box was from a pair of trainers I didn't recognise, and I was about to throw it away when I noticed the weight – not empty and not full – and the sound of papers shuffling inside. I sat down cross-legged on the floor and set the box in front of me.

Inside I found a photograph of a girl I couldn't remember having ever met. The picture was a little blurry, and the girl was some distance from the photographer. She leaned against a wall in front of a pale grey smudge of sea. She was smiling, and her hair was caught in the wind. It was difficult to tell when the picture was taken. It could have been last year, or it could have been fifteen years ago. Could the box have been here when we moved in? Surely we would have noticed it. The longer I stared, the longer I thought the girl in the photo looked a little like me; but I didn't recognise the clothes she wore, and her hair had a different tone, catching the light in a way that mine never would. It crossed my mind that this might be a picture of my birth mother, or of myself in an alternate reality. Or perhaps clothes and hair were all that really distinguished me from other women. I laid the photograph down on the carpet and took out the next sheet.

It was an offer letter for a job in Edinburgh. I knew that Owen had a few friends there. I could remember him speaking about them, but I could not remember anything about him applying for a job there; we had certainly never discussed moving to Scotland. The letter was not dated. Perhaps it was just a coincidence that the recipient of the letter shared Owen's last name. No first name was mentioned. I looked up the business name at Companies House, but it had been shut down a year previously; I could find no record of it anywhere else online. I put the letter down on top of the photograph.

Next was a printout; a few sheets of A4 paper stapled together. I flipped through them. It was a brochure for a flat that was available to rent. It had been folded a couple of times, but it didn't look particularly old, definitely not older than our relationship. The flat was in Manchester. I googled the address and the listing was still online, the flat was still available. I knew it was possible that the listing was a duplicate, an old advert used again, but this was of no comfort to me. Unless this box did not belong to Owen.

Although I had been convinced that he would leave me one day, there had never been a time when Owen could feasibly have been looking for a flat without me. I knew he had a life outside of me – I wasn't happy about it – but could his secret life really have been this extreme? How long could he have been considering leaving me? How long had he been planning?

I put the papers back in the box and took it to the bath. I took a lighter to one corner. The flame lapped at the laminated cardboard, singeing the edge, which smoked thickly. I dropped the flaming box into the tub and watched it shrivel and crackle. After a minute or so, I turned on the tap and soaked the box, ripping the sheets of mushy paper until they meant nothing. I dropped the sloppy mess into the bathroom bin and rinsed the meagre ashes away. I stared at the tub for a long time.

The box of betrayals should have torn me apart, but as I sat there thinking it over, I couldn't bring myself to be upset or angry. I was a little confused about what I had seen, I wanted to understand what Owen had been thinking, but I felt almost nothing. Perhaps he was thinking about making an escape, trying on different identities, but wasn't that exactly what I had been doing? Wasn't that what we were all doing? I wished

I could show him how much I had changed. Our relationship could have been so different.

◆

I would never usually sit at the bar. It felt intrusive, watching people do their jobs. I was afraid that – if they did not resent the pressure of my presence – they might try to talk to me. What would I say? People trickled through the door in ones and twos, so that the place felt empty until suddenly it was full. With the tables all occupied, a woman had no choice but to sit down beside me at the bar. She was young, but her face carried an expression I had only seen in older women. She was not afraid to be here. I wondered if my expression had begun to display such an inherent confidence, now that I carried within me the spirit of a man.

When the woman blinked, she kept her eyes closed for a beat too long. She slumped over the bar with a sigh when her drink arrived, staring into it as if it might hold the answer to her questioning frown. A curled tendril of hair trailed into a sticky mess on the surface of the bar, and when she turned her head to look at me the tendril whipped across her face and stuck to her cheek adorably. I dropped my head out of habit, although I didn't feel shy or intimidated by this girl. I couldn't remember the last time another girl had not seemed like a threat to me, but now this woman felt like an opportunity for which I did not, could not, begrudge Owen.

I couldn't remember the last time I had really lusted after someone. I had tried to be sexy for Owen's benefit, but I had been so busy stressing out about his perception of me that I had all but blocked out my own sexuality. I suppose lust had never seemed like an elementary part of my identity; it was more like an impossible bar that I was always trying to reach.

But as I watched the girl from the corner of my eye, my stomach dropped; my mouth ran dry, I became conscious of my nipples rubbing against the fabric of my T-shirt. I uncrossed my legs and crossed them again, squirming a little on the bar stool.

She glanced over at me and turned away quickly when she was satisfied that I was not staring at her, unaware of what she had awoken in me. In my periphery, I could see her gently fingering the outside of her glass, marking patterns in the condensation and watching as the drips smashed through them. My fingers floated to my lips.

I had been with Owen for so long that I hadn't really had many opportunities to explore my own desires outside of him.

When I came in earlier that evening, the bartender had asked me if I wanted him to change the channel. There was no one else around to watch the game, he said, and he wasn't fussed about this one. I said no and called him 'mate', just to roll the word around on my tongue. I nodded when he placed my drink on the bar in front of me. Since then, the bartender and I had lingered in the kind of silent camaraderie I had always admired in men. I stared at the game on the screen as if I cared about or understood it, basking in the sense of belonging that my exchange with the bartender afforded me. Now, two hours later, the news was on and I watched a sensible and friendly grandfather of a man reading headlines beside a woman – twenty years his junior – whose smile appeared to be permanent in spite of all the wrongs it was her job to explain.

The girl beside me had moved her sticky fingers into her hair, working them independently through the knots while she stared down into her drink. I wondered what she was doing here. Was it normal to come to a bar and drink on your own? I had never had the confidence to try it before.

When she turned to look at me again, I smiled, and she faltered before smiling back crookedly. She dropped her head and shifted in her seat so that, ever so slightly, her back was turned to me.

Soon she was joined by another girl and together they drank, touching one another's arms and cheeks and hair. The first girl watched me while she whispered something in the second girl's ear, and together they exploded into giggles.

I wasn't sure what I had wanted to happen that evening. Perhaps I was jealous of the two girls' open and energised lust, or maybe I just found them annoying, returning to my natural bitter state. I hadn't much considered the effect of the situation on my sexuality, and over the course of the evening I had grown uncertain of my attractions. What I *was* sure of was my lack of guilt regarding my own honest handling of my desires. I allowed myself to admit my own excitement at the prospect of exploring myself further.

I finished my fourth glass of wine and left the bar. I headed in the direction of the flat, but when I reached it, I carried on walking. I walked for a long time until the streets became quieter, lined with houses where curtains were drawn and in which children slept. I found myself on the narrow street where Owen and I had met for the second time, at a party after which we had become inseparable. My stomach lurched, and I wondered if that was what it felt like when you were pregnant and the baby moved, sort of like the gurgle of vomit before it hits the throat.

The moon, like me, was full. It seemed as if we were both about to burst. The windows of the house were dark, but a white sign glowed by the front door; it was for sale. The windows were dusty, and I leaned in close to see inside. I staggered backwards and nearly lost my footing at the sight of the glowing forms. I knew almost immediately that what I saw were not ghosts but furniture covered with sheets; still, I drew a few deep breaths before cupping my hands around my eyes and leaning in once more.

I heard distant laughter coming from inside. I pulled my coat tighter around myself and placed my hand gently on the doorknob. I hadn't intended to go inside, but the door was open. I couldn't remember whether I had turned the knob or not. It had started to rain – I could hear fat droplets explode on the leaves in the trees before I could feel them – and I stepped inside instinctively. The wind tore through the house and the sheets rippled, but I wasn't startled this time. I found myself surrounded by party guests, furniture ghosts. I felt safe with them looming around me. I pulled the sheet off one particularly tall ghost and put my ear to its chest. The grandfather clock – whose incongruence Owen and I had bonded over – ticked out a heartbeat, and for a moment I felt his arms pull me in closer. I closed my eyes and rested in his grip for a long time. I heard him scream and then he screamed again and then he continued to scream. It was eleven p.m. and I recoiled from the clock.

I moved into the kitchen, drawn to the fridge, which was oddly still on, humming lightly in life. My mouth watered as I opened the door. A rancid waft hit me in the face and I saw two rotten steaks on a plate covered with cling film. I wrinkled my nose and pulled my head away without moving my feet. I staggered to the sink and dry heaved until I was sure nothing would come up.

A shuffling sound in the next room drew me through the house's coronary artery and into its heart. I sunk into an old family-softened armchair. I closed my eyes, and when I opened them again a fat brown rat stood in front of me in the bare centre of the room. When it caught my eye, it wondered languorously to the doorway and stopped to look back at me. It wanted me to follow, so I did.

The rat stopped in front of a cupboard door. I opened it and the rat hopped in. On a hook hung the coat that Owen had worn when we first met. I hadn't seen it for some time, and suspected that he had left it here by accident. I reached out gratefully and put it on. He wasn't much bigger than me and it fit snugly over my own coat, an extra skin to keep him in.

In the next room, all but one of the dining chairs was covered. I sat down on the uncovered one. I rested my forearms on the table so they sat at right angles to my torso, my palms face down. 'Where are you?' I asked the darkness.

♦

When I got back, the flat was hot and swampy. My head was foggy with wine and my motivations were blurred. I knew no one could hear me, but I spoke out loud.

'Owen,' I called, 'I need you. What are you doing? Come out.'

I held my breath and listened, tried to imagine the absorption in reverse. What sound would it make? Would he crack open my ribs, or poke a finger out through my belly button? Would he ooze out through my pores like sweat or pus? Or maybe it would be a birth of sorts, my body contracting to create a natural opening for him to squeeze through, bloody and naked and crying. *Imagine birthing a man that size.* Didn't I hear somewhere that pelvic bones moved during pregnancy? He would split me open, using my bones as levers to break through my flesh. I shuddered and reeled my thoughts in. I knew he wasn't coming back, and under the circumstances I had imagined, I wouldn't want him to. I needed to stick to my plan and move on.

I sat on the sofa with my laptop. I turned the TV on and then turned it off again. The sound was jarring. I needed to work in silence. My brain was loud enough already. I entered the address and then I started to type.

I have a spare room going in my 2-bed flat. I'd like to live with someone clean and interesting. I'm late 20s, work at the council and I like writing. Would be good to live with someone else with a 9–5 type job and an interest in films, books, music, etc. To move in asap.

I hated what I had written but I didn't know what else to say about myself. There must have been a time in my life when I had felt confident in my interests, in my ability to be interesting, but now I was just a list of demographics, potentially a murderer, definitely a monster. I remember feeling – once, a long time ago – that my personality was an asset, but as I sat there that night and looked at the words I had written, I realised that I had become a stereotype, or worse, a template of a woman, ready to fill out with talent and quirks, just waiting.

I took photos of the flat on my phone. It was not nearly bright enough and the photos were dark and blurry. I uploaded them anyway and then pasted in the description. I didn't include my phone number, which would be obscured by the website anyway. I couldn't be bothered to speak to anyone.

When I got into bed, I could feel the warmth in Owen's side. I got up and checked the bathroom. It was empty. I stood on the landing and listened. I could almost hear the sound of him biting his nails, a sound that I only ever heard when I was in a different room. What other habits did he hide from me? I tried to follow the sound, but every time I focused, it stopped, or moved to a different space. I got back into bed, turned off the lamp, and looked at my phone: my nightly ritual.

My stomach loosened and dropped when I saw Helena pop up in my feed. A writer I followed had liked something she had posted. My thumb hovered over her avatar and seemed to press down of its own accord. I wanted so desperately for her feed to be busy and banal, but it was sparse and considered and not at all braggy. I felt a warm spark similar to the one I had felt when I watched her on New Year's Eve, but stronger this time. I scrolled through her posts, and as I did, the warm spot grew and I flushed with excitement. It wasn't the content of her posts so much as the fact that they were innocuous now; cute and considered. By the time I realised I had accidentally liked one of the posts, she was already following me. Blood pounded through my skull. When I saw the new message icon, I dropped my phone.

Hey Allison! How's it going? Haven't seen you or Owen around in a while. Hope everything's okay? H x

Fuck. I was an idiot. I'd already told several conflicting versions of the story to different people. There was no way I was telling Helena the truth, but I needed to limit the lies so I could manage them more easily in the future.

I think he's staying with some family, I'm not really sure.

I took a deep breath and wrote another message.

We broke up.

Are you okay?

Her reply was instant, like she was genuinely shocked, or already knew.

I'm okay. He didn't tell you?

I haven't spoken to him since NYE. Do you want to meet up for a coffee soon?

I didn't reply.

I checked my emails before I put my phone down. I had four replies to my housemate ad already. I felt sick.

SIXTEEN

I was still thinking about Helena when I woke. I had dreamed about her all night, and although I couldn't recall anything specific, I woke feeling as if I had been wrapped around her for days. In the first moments between sleep and wakefulness, I was certain of her warmth beside me, which called to a corresponding warmth growing within me. I remembered exchanging messages with her the previous night, and I read them back to solidify the truth of my memory. I thought of all the women I had disregarded for fear that growing closer to them would give Owen the opportunity to do the same; as if by befriending the women I admired, I was opening the door for him to leave me. Perhaps my fear of beautiful, clever, funny and kind women stemmed from a perceived inability to love them as I innately wanted to. I liked boys, I thought, but hadn't I really only liked one boy?

I was confused. I couldn't face the prospect of a housemate that morning. Regret washed over me as I recalled the advert. I had been hasty. I stared at the coffee as it percolated. It was bitter; I must have left it to brew for some time.

Things seemed better when I wasn't in bed, which was odd, because bed had always been a safe space for me. Whenever I felt sad, or anxious, I would curl up beneath the weight of my duvet and drift away. And even if I couldn't disappear into that soft nothingness of sleep, I would find myself in worlds created by my mind and nothing else. Even when my dreams were bad, as they often were, they were rarely accompanied by anxiety comparable to that which I felt when I was awake. Every morning I woke with a deep feeling of dread which was rinsed away by the first half hour of the day. And so, that day, after I had showered and dressed, my plan for a housemate began to seem, once again, like a good idea. I needed to rebuild my life, if only to prevent the truth from getting out.

I had just sat down to start replying to the emails when I heard a slamming shatter from the kitchen. I had become accustomed to strange happenings in the flat, but this sound was violent, an explosion of shards: an attack, or a warning. A scream like none I had ever heard reverberated through the flat. *This is it*, I thought, *it's finally happening*, although I would have been hard pressed to explain what exactly I thought was going on. I sprung up and followed the sound. The kitchen had a doorway but no door – my landlady's attempt at open-plan living, I supposed – so that, as I approached, slivers of the room revealed themselves to me. As anyone who's ever watched a horror film will appreciate, an empty room from which sounds emanate is infinitely more terrifying when it is revealed in fractions. There's something about wholeness that makes us feel safe. If it hadn't been for the smash and the scream, the sounds that followed may have made sense, but it was the not knowing that drove me forward in fear. The inhuman screams, I soon realised, were the pained mewlings of my neighbour's cat, who was panicking in a puddle of broken glass and china and blood. When he looked up and saw me, he gazed directly into my eyes and howled again. The kitchen window was open. I hadn't opened it.

It wasn't as bad as it looked. I swept up the glass first, but looking back it seems my priorities were confused. When I was satisfied with the condition of the floor, I picked up the cat. He hissed at me and flexed his claws. He howled in pain and then went limp in my arms. In the bathroom, I pulled pieces of glass out of his paws with tweezers. He woke with a hiss as I dabbed the cuts with antiseptic wipes from the first aid box. It was not the first time I had patched this cat up; my neighbour was a less than ideal owner. The cat licked his paws and started to retch dryly. I thought about bandaging him up, but I didn't think I could bear to see him like that. I left him on the bath mat to recover.

I sent the same email to everyone who had replied to my ad, inviting them to come over the next day. I didn't think I could afford to be fussy. As I typed, the cat traipsed bloody footprints across the floor and over the sofa. I didn't shout at him or shoo him; it seemed appropriate somehow, as if he might be printing out Owen's footprints, a sort of feline Morse code, marking the areas that Owen roamed alongside me, bodiless.

I allowed myself to be excited at the prospect of introducing someone new into my life. Wherever Owen's consciousness was now, I couldn't see him, and if I couldn't see him, he was as good as gone. A new flatmate would be someone to start again with, someone who could get me out of this mess. I wonder now if I got what I wanted.

◆

In spite of the number of responses I had for the housemate ad, Martin was the only one to reply to my invite. He was tall, taller than Owen, but would have benefitted from losing an inch or two; his head rolled around on his neck like a marble on top of a snooker cue. I worried that it might roll right off and shatter on the floor.

'Marble,' I said.

'Martin,' said the small-headed man.

'That's what I said,' I told him, as I gestured for him to come in. He pressed his lips together. I realised that he was smiling.

'How's it going,' I said, but I forgot the question mark, so the words just floated there, unanchored between us.

Martin said something, but I didn't listen, focusing instead on a hairline so far forward that I began to question my belief in natural selection. He was looking at me expectantly, so I said, 'Yes,' and nodded. His frown didn't do him any favours in the Neanderthal department, but it did inform me that I had given the wrong response.

'Did you come far?' I asked in an effort to save the conversation. Martin unhooked his jaw like a snake and I felt deeply afraid of what would come out of his mouth next; it seemed less likely to be words than some horrific extension of his gullet that would jut deep into my throat and suck out my internal organs.

'Not really,' he said, 'just around the corner.'

I showed him around the flat as quickly as I could.

◆

I had never been good in any 'getting-to-know-you' scenario. Every time someone asked my name, where I was from, where I had been to school, I froze. No matter how much time passed, how much space I put between myself and the day-care centre, I was still afraid that people would find out who I was, what was wrong with me.

Fresher's week was a nightmare. I didn't start drinking until it was legal, and I had never taken drugs, so I spent the week drinking alcopops and coconut rum and saying, 'Nah, not tonight, thanks,' whenever anyone offered me a pill. The music in the club was violating, the bass sinking and rising in my throat.

At school, I had forged a group of friends who had found my frosty detachment appealing. I had no trouble with boys back then; they had already decided that women were somehow crazy and demanding, but that I was different. And I *was* different, but only in that I was traumatised and insecure and I created barriers that made them feel like I was one of them. I did nothing to correct them.

My body felt all wrong as I stood there awkwardly on the dance floor, swirling a straw around in my plastic cup and trying to move my knees to a rhythm I couldn't find. I wore big, plastic earrings that made my earlobes droop; my dress was bandage tight; my asymmetrical haircut too bold and desperate in this new environment. I kept flicking my fringe out of my eyes and wishing I could turn myself inside out.

My new flatmate, Laura, came back from the bar with a snakebite and black. I didn't know what it was. She laughed when she saw me spit the sickly purple liquid back into the glass. Laura was saying something, but I couldn't hear what, so I just watched her mouth opening and closing, and when it stopped I made a surprised face and raised my eyebrows. She paused, confused, but I just smiled at her like an idiot, so she carried on speaking. At one point, she pulled me close and said, 'Don't look now, but those guys are looking at us.'

Of course, I looked, and I saw two men wearing almost identical pastel-coloured shirts tucked into indigo bootcut jeans with pointy black loafers. Laura followed my gaze and started making eyes at them. They were coming over. I made a smoking gesture with my fingers and walked past them to get outside.

The smoking area was big, but it was raining, so everyone was huddled under a slim awning that dangled from the club's exterior. I rummaged in my bag for a lighter, a cigarette drooping from my bottom lip.

'Do you need a light?'

I looked up and there he was, an angel with a sweeping black fringe. He flicked his hair out of his eyes and dug around in the pocket of his low-slung skinny jeans. He reached out to light the cigarette for me, but I plucked the lighter out of his hand and did it myself. A girl called out, 'Owen!' and he raised his eyebrows, shrugged and walked off. I still held the lighter tightly in my palm as I went back in to find Laura.

She was on the dance floor, illuminated from below by the multicoloured light-up tiles. She was grinding with one of the bootcut boys, her hands resting on the chest of his half-unbuttoned shirt. If I had known then what I know now, I would have dragged her out of there. We might have even remained friends. But if I had done that, I wouldn't have met Owen. I used this to justify myself for years after, but it doesn't really cut it any more. I have failed too many people to be forgiven.

I woke up in his bed, but it took me a minute to realise that I was not in my own room, itself not yet familiar to me. I tried to swallow but my mouth was so dry that my throat just folded in on itself. I stroked the inside of my mouth with my sandy tongue to lubricate it.

The figure next to me was breathing heavily, not quite snoring. I shimmied down to the end of the bed and flopped out like a fish. My clothes were in a neat pile on a chair; in the years to come, I would get used to Owen tidying up after me like this. I got dressed as quietly as I could. On the desk was a photo of Owen with a woman who I thought was his mother. I stifled a scoff and picked my way between the empty cans and unpacked boxes to the door.

I had assumed that I would never see him again, and I congratulated myself on my fresher's week conquest. I felt that I had acted like a normal teenager. I met him again at a party a few days later, and we had been together ever since.

◆

When I think back to the arguments we had, they blend together. The amount of times he said he didn't want to go to sleep angry, and the amount of times I told him that was ridiculous, a turn of phrase, a cliché. I would turn my back on him and fall into sleep easily. I would never feel guilty that he wasn't able to do the same. I could never get it into my head that my actions affected him, although everything I said and did was directly related to him. I had assumed my own feelings were wrong and that nobody would dwell on the hurtful things I said and did, because everyone else understood some secret to life that I was missing. I hadn't realised I was being horrible, because I had thought I was too insignificant to actually have an effect on people.

I remember waking up the morning after a particularly unmemorable argument, the taste of blood on my tongue, the sour prickle of an open-mouthed sleep, sinuses too blocked with tears to breathe normally. I remember how I had tried to swallow away the gummy throat without letting Owen know that I was awake, swallowing over and over until my nose and throat and mouth felt connected again. I remember the way a weighted coat of mascara locked my lashes together. I took comfort in the darkness behind my own eyelids, dreading the gravel of crumbled make-up that would scratch at my eyes when I opened them. I remember holding my breath in imitation sleep, not knowing whether I should breathe louder or quieter or faster or slower. I could always tell when Owen was pretending to be asleep, his body would be too rigid to be resting. A shift in his breath would let me know that he was thinking about us or waiting to find out how I would justify myself, my insecurity, my anger. My muscles, spring-loaded, tightened in anticipation of his touch. I longed for that warmth as he moved closer, bringing me to the cusp of comfort, and I cursed myself that I rolled away, opting instead for the cusp of the mattress. I remember how he rolled away on a sigh and it felt as if I was connected to him by a thread of dental floss; the fresh, minty pull of him that I resisted in favour of my own stale, fetid breath reflected back at me within the mask of the duvet.

I know the way I shunned him in my self-loathing was exhausting. I know that I dragged him over sharp corners that he thought had long since been filed down; he worked so hard to smooth them, to heal those slashes in myself that let the dark in.

SEVENTEEN

Elliott opened the door.

'Oh,' he said, followed by an uncomfortable pause. 'Allison! Come in!' I knew he hadn't expected me to actually come, that I was only invited as a courtesy. I had never been to one of these things without Owen before. I shouldn't be here. But where else was I supposed to go? And if Cara was here at Elliott's party – as she was almost certain to be – perhaps Natalie would be too. I was set on moving on with my life. I thought I might even be able to piece my friendship with Natalie back together. I would know what to say this time. I would be able to find the words to make things right, just like Owen always did. I followed Elliott through to the kitchen.

'I'm so sorry to hear about...' Elliott trailed off. 'Are you okay?'

I nodded and tried to smile but only succeeded in stretching my lips into a thin horizontal line.

'He's not here,' said Elliott with urgency, as if he had just realised that might be a concern for me. 'Is he still with his family?'

There was no need to lie. 'I don't know.'

His sad smile reflected my own straight lips. 'Have you heard from him?' he asked.

'I spoke to his mum,' I said.

Elliott opened his mouth to ask more but the doorbell rang, and he rushed to answer it. I poured myself a glass of wine and headed for the bifold doors.

The party was in Elliott's parents' house. It was a four-storey town house, a bit like the one in which I now rented a single floor. It was a beautiful house. I'd been here before, but always with Owen. It felt strange to be here now, as if I was somehow spying on him.

The bifold doors opened onto a multi-tiered garden with a pond, a barbeque patio, a sheltered area with cushioned seats and a summer house. I had always resented Elliott for his parents' wealth, but it didn't really bother me now. I headed straight for the sheltered seats, which was where I always hid at Elliott's parties.

'Allison?' someone asked as I walked straight past them. I paused. It was Cara.

'Hey,' I grunted.

'Hey! I'm so glad you came,' she said. Her eyes wrinkled into two little crescent moons and the corners of her lips twitched.

'Is Natalie—' I started.

'CARA!' someone squealed from inside the house. 'You have to see this!'

Cara rolled her eyes.

'Go,' I said, 'I'm fine, we'll catch up later?' I didn't mean it, but I had learned what I needed to give people in order for them to leave me alone.

'Sorry,' said Cara, 'I'd better go see to that. I'll catch you later, yeah?' I nodded, and Cara patted me on the shoulder and went back into the house.

I'd always made a big deal of not wanting to be touched. 'I'm just not really a hugger,' I'd tell people. Natalie and Maggie always hugged me anyway, and I always squirmed, but it wasn't a genuine response. I wished that Cara would hug me, even though the reason she didn't was because she was respecting the boundaries I had set.

I walked through the garden and sat down on a cushioned bench, hidden from the patio behind a wooden pillar. There were lanterns strung around, but I didn't turn them on. It was cold but the dark wrapped itself around me like a blanket. I lit a cigarette. I had come to this party to be around other people, but now that I was here, I had isolated myself.

I had learned this habit at parties with Owen. Back when everyone used to smoke, we would congregate outside in a big group that no outsider could penetrate. But as we got older, people started to quit, or cut back, and they became more interested in other people, people we didn't already know. Owen and his friends would mingle inside, and I would sit in the garden and smoke and look at my phone. I knew I was cold, moody, unapproachable, but I was scared. What if people laughed at me? What if I couldn't think of anything to say? If I didn't try, I couldn't kid myself into thinking that people might like me.

I heard the bifold doors slide open and closed, and then voices on the patio.

'She must've gone back inside,' a familiar voice said, 'thank god.'

'Come on, she's not that bad,' said a voice I didn't recognise.

'Oh, I know, she's having a hard time, but she's never liked me. It's just awkward.'

'Yeah, I know what you mean, I—'

I coughed, and they stopped talking. I couldn't bear to hear what they were going to say about me. I held my breath and stayed hidden behind the pillar for all of our sakes. The voices started up again a few seconds later, quieter this time.

So, Cara felt the same way about me as I felt about her. I'd always suspected that people were talking about me behind my back, but I'd never heard it before. I had imagined it would feel worse, but Cara's reasoning made sense. Owen had always dealt well with criticism.

The bifold doors opened and closed again and I was alone in the garden. I was cold, and I had finished my wine, but I waited for a larger group of people to come outside before I slipped back into the house, unnoticed.

◆

I found Elliott in the kitchen with his sister – whose name I couldn't remember – and a couple of the flappy-trouser boys from the New Year's Eve party.

'I heard about you and Owen,' said Elliott's sister. 'I'm sorry, are you doing okay?'

'Yeah,' I said, and then I said it again with more emphasis, '*yeah*, I am actually. It's weird, but I'm feeling good.' I knew that it sounded more like I was trying to convince myself, and in a way, I suppose I was. I *had* felt good, but the feeling was slipping away. I knew that I needed some kind of resolution, something to mark the end of this episode in my life and allow me to move forwards, but I had no idea what that would be.

'What happened?' asked Elliott's sister, and I wasn't just talking to her any more, but to everyone in the kitchen. They were all staring at me like they knew exactly what had happened; but they couldn't, they were probably just thirsty for gossip. 'I mean, you don't have to talk about it if you don't want.' She didn't mean that, but she wouldn't push it if I was evasive. This was my chance to seal my story.

'We just had a big fight, on New Year's Eve,' I said. I took a deep breath. I had rehearsed this line but it still hurt. 'He said he wasn't sure he loved me any more. And then he just left.'

No one said anything.

'I haven't seen him since,' I said and shrugged. 'His mum said he's staying with some relatives.'

'Oh… I'm sorry, Allison,' said Elliott, although I had no idea why he should be the one to apologise. 'Maybe he just needs some time?'

'Yeah, maybe,' I said.

◆

Cara, Elliott's sister and the flappy-trouser boys wanted to play a drinking game, but Elliott didn't, and neither did I. I went outside to smoke again, and he followed me.

'Can I have one?' he asked.

'I thought you quit?'

'I did.'

I handed over a cigarette and a lighter.

'Thanks.' He lit up and took a deep drag with his eyes closed. He pushed the smoke out slowly, performing satisfaction.

'How are you holding up?' he said, opening his eyes. 'Really?'

'I'm okay,' I said, 'it's… weird, but it's okay.'

'You should try talking to Cara,' he said.

I smiled but didn't say anything.

'Yeah, I know she's not your favourite person, but she'd be a really good friend if you'd let her.'

The bifold doors opened.

'Is anyone out here?' called a voice.

'Over here!' said Elliott.

Footsteps approached, and Cara came into view.

'Hey!' she said. 'Oh Al, I don't suppose I could have a cigarette, could I?'

Elliott stood up. 'I'd better go back in,' he said. He put a hand on Cara's waist as he walked past her and back towards the house. I waited until he had gone inside before I said anything. Cara lit the cigarette I had given her.

'How's Natalie?' I asked.

'She's good. Her and Michael broke up, but she's good.'

'Good,' I echoed.

We sat in silence for a minute, passing the wine glass back and forth.

'Cara?' I asked. 'Do you like me?' I don't know where it came from. I had been thinking about Natalie, about what I could say to Cara to help me get my best friend back. I had no idea what I was going to say until I said it.

Cara choked on her cigarette and I handed her my glass of wine. She took a swig and cleared her throat.

'Of course I do, why do you ask that?'

'Oh, come on,' I said, 'honestly.'

'Honestly?' she took another drag and exhaled slowly. 'Okay, well. Look. It's just. You're not exactly that easy to get on with.'

I nodded. 'Yeah, I get that,' I said.

She loosened up a little, took another drag of the cigarette, another sip of my wine.

'I've always thought you seem really cool, but like kind of cold?'

I looked at her and raised an eyebrow. She laughed.

'You know what I mean. You're always so… aloof. Look, I know stuff is probably pretty difficult for you right now. Owen's being a total dick, he hasn't even messaged Elliott. And I know the whole Natalie thing probably doesn't make it easier. But she'll be fine soon, she loves you. And in the meantime, I'm here if you need a friend, okay?'

'Seriously?' I asked. Cara laughed again.

'Obviously, yes. I just always thought you didn't like me, that's all. Here.' She picked my phone up off the wall and started to type in her number. How did I not already have it?

'Text me, okay, we'll get a drink?'

'Okay. Thanks, Cara.'

'Shut up, let's get more wine.'

◆

The party was still going strong when I left. It was only around midnight, but I stumbled a bit as I walked home. I couldn't believe how easy it had been.

◆

I nearly fell down the stairs when I got to my flat. The front door was open. The door to the street had been deadlocked, but the door to my flat was ajar. I pushed it with one finger as though it was dirty. It creaked open a little more.

It was dark inside, and I took tiny, shuffling steps through the door, slapping the light switch with my palm as soon as I was in.

'Hello?' I said.

Nothing.

I ran into the kitchen, my bedroom, the spare room, the bathroom, and then back to the front door which I slammed shut. Then I went back through each room, opening cupboards, checking behind doors and under beds. No one was there. Nothing was missing.

EIGH——TEEN

When Maggie messaged me to say that she had a friend looking for somewhere to live, it felt like everything might be falling into place. It was one of those moments where my world, which had been so close to collapsing in on itself, began to restore its equilibrium.

'She's a bit of a hippy,' Maggie said in her message, 'but she's so sweet and warm, you'll love her.'

Getting a flatmate didn't make me feel like I was moving on from Owen. Or if it did, it was more that I was moving on after an appropriate amount of time. If there was an appropriate recovery period after consuming your partner, I had calculated it to be around five weeks.

Absorbing Owen had started to feel more normal, a traumatic but natural phenomenon with an overall net positive outcome.

A bit like giving birth or finding faith after contracting a serious disease. I couldn't feel Owen physically within me. I couldn't have a conversation with him. I wasn't possessed. I had not *entirely* lost touch with the absurdity of the situation, but I was accepting it like a scar or a new haircut.

I glanced out the window at the exact moment Odile opened my front gate. When I told her so, she said, 'It must be a sign!' and laughed. Odile was probably around Maggie's age with pronounced crow's feet that made her look like she was smiling even when she wasn't.

I offered Odile a cup of tea and watched her reflection in the kettle as I waited for the water to boil. She looked around the kitchen, moving with her entire body to soak everything in. She was so grounded, like her soul – rather than just her feet – was connected with the kitchen lino. She swayed a little, a tree that had taken root in the flat hundreds of years ago. She belonged there so much more than I did.

I wanted to show her around, to assert my power over my habitat, but I just stood in the living room and pointed to the rooms that branched off it – kitchen, bathroom… When I pointed to my room she nodded politely and stayed put, and when I pointed to the spare room she wandered inside as if it were already hers. I stayed in the living room, watching her.

'It's perfect,' she said, and it was.

We sat down and talked about the details. I told her I had chosen a green energy supplier, which I thought would please her, and she responded kindly to my vanity. She told me about the bookshop where she worked, how it didn't pay much, which was why she couldn't live on her own but was much happier with company anyway. I told her that the room was available immediately and she said that was great, she was staying with a friend at the moment and she didn't want to outstay her welcome there.

I tried to explain my situation further.

'I was living here with my—'

'Oh honey, there's no need. I can see you've been through great trauma, you don't need to explain yourself.'

I smiled weakly. 'You can move in whenever you're ready,' I said. I wondered how much of my story she already knew from Maggie.

◆

Owen and I had been living in the flat for less than three years. After university, we lived in a shared house with a bunch of people, most of whom we hadn't spoken to since. We got a tiny one-bed flat when I started working at the council. About two years before he quit his job, Owen got a pay rise, and we moved here. At that point, we thought we had put in enough time at work to earn the right to a moderate life. Back then, I thought we had already paid the price of comfort.

I had great plans for the spare room. I thought the extra space would be reflected within me, as if I might be able to grow into it. I bought a yoga mat and a vintage desk. I used neither, but at first it didn't matter. Just the existence of a spare room was enough to prove something, to prove how far we had come.

When we moved in, we were just playing grown-ups. We had a loving, long-term relationship, a flat with a spare room, respectable jobs. We nearly got a dog, but decided to wait, to give ourselves something to look forward to. People knew us as a unit – Allison and Owen, Owen and Allison. To me, this was a great success. Whenever anybody invited Owen out, it was assumed that the invitation was extended to me, and vice versa. Sometimes I wasn't invited – 'Boys' night,' Owen would say –

and I gave myself a proverbial pat on the back for coping on my own, although mostly I ended up finding someone else to hang out with. On the nights when I found no replacement for him, and had been forced to spend the evening alone, I would drink in front of the TV so that my soberness would not sour his return. When he asked me in the morning how my night had been, I would tell him it had been lovely, peaceful, that he should go out more often. I didn't tell him about my crippling doubt, the arguments I ran over in my head, how I had planned exactly what I would say when he revealed there had been someone else, how I had to push so hard against his body in bed to fight the magnetic repulsiveness of it. I tried to play it cool. For a while, that was almost enough.

But it wasn't long until we weren't playing any more. Somewhere along the line, we started to grow up. It was difficult when Owen went freelance. It started with the bills: he couldn't pay on time; his clients were late on their invoices. I paid his share of the rent for the first two months, and I resented him for it. And then he was working late, replying to emails and making phone calls in the evenings and on weekends. His life was more important than mine, his job was more fulfilling, his talent more promising, and just like that I became a version of the mother I always feared becoming, Owen sucking the life out of me, growing better and brighter as I collapsed in on myself. I wonder now if that was what he was always looking for – a mother figure. And if so, did he not know me well enough to know that I was not maternal in the least, that I would quickly come to begrudge caring for him as he superseded me in life?

◆

I've often wondered if there's anything as awful as getting to know somebody. It's like a puzzle – intermittently fun and frustrating.

No matter how careful you are, there are always pieces missing. I was always frightened by the notion that I would never truly know someone, and I would never truly be known. Because what if you gave away too much in return for too little? What if they didn't need you as much as you needed them? What if the balance of my life was well and truly fucked? What if I had got it all wrong? And perhaps even more frightening was the thought that if I *was* getting it all wrong, I wouldn't even realise. I would have nothing to compare it with. I had no idea what right looked like.

Like a jigsaw puzzle, Owen's value to me had always lain in his fragmentation, and the more I tried to piece him together, the more I realised how many pieces had been lost, or were simply not available to me, and I became distraught and increasingly lonely. I wanted everything he had, and I was happy to sacrifice the remaining scraps of my identity for it.

◆

While I had gained a flatmate, I had lost a valid excuse for not quitting my job. As it turned out, quitting was not as hard as I had imagined.

When I went into work on Monday, the HR manager, Karen, cornered me and asked for a word.

'Allison, how are you?' she asked as she closed the door to her office. I knew that the nature of her work required her to have a space of privacy, and I should have been grateful that we were not having this discussion in front of Jean and the others, but I wasn't.

I said I was fine, in the hope that being vague would get me out of there faster, but Karen wasn't having any of it.

'I'm glad to hear it,' she purred with faux sympathy, her eyes two little half-moons in her sarcastic face. 'Darren's been worried. He has big plans for you, you know?'

'Actually, Karen,' I started, before switching the pitch of my voice to sound less aggressive, more assertive, 'I was hoping to talk to you about something.'

Karen raised her eyebrows and her lips made a little lower-case 'o', but she didn't say anything.

'Give me a second,' I said and rushed out of the room.

Back at my desk, Jean was staring at me strangely. I ignored her, fumbled with my computer and waited by the printer for the paper to slip out. I snatched the paper from the printer tray as I headed back into Karen's office.

'What's this?' she asked.

'It's my notice,' I said.

'Oh,' said Karen, putting the paper down on her desk without reading it. 'Do you have something else lined up?' she asked.

'No,' I said, and for once I didn't feel the need to explain myself any further. I wasn't withholding out of anger; it was none of her business what I was going to do with my life, and even if I had known, I didn't owe her an explanation. I didn't owe anyone anything. Still, she waited for me to continue, and when I didn't she said, 'Is everything okay, Allison?'

'Yes,' I said, 'brilliant.' It sounded sarcastic, but in the moment, I meant it. I *was* brilliant. My life had turned a corner. Sure, I missed Owen, but I was a better person now; confident, more grateful, more ambitious. I was moving on, getting a new housemate, and I felt confident that this would change the atmosphere in the flat, bring about the peace I needed in which to settle into my new self.

◆

I took a long lunch, no longer afraid of being fired, and meandered through the streets to find the shop where Odile worked. I walked slowly, moving in the general direction I knew the shop to be in, with little regard for the time I was wasting. It was time that didn't belong to me anyway. The door was plastered with endorsement stickers from various organisations and an 'open' sign. Wind chimes jangled as I pushed my way in.

'Allison!' Odile beamed out at me from a cloud of incense smoke. 'I was just thinking of you!'

I smiled. 'I've brought the keys,' I said. After a beat, I added, 'To the flat.' The atmosphere in the shop was so oppressive that it seemed to squeeze the extra words out of me.

'Wonderful,' said Odile. 'You have time for a cup of tea, don't you?' She disappeared behind a beaded curtain before I could answer. I glanced around at the Dymo printed labels stuck to the shelves: Esoteric Teachings, Hermetic Arts, Paranormal, Satanism, Sufism, Taoism, Yoga. I did my best to avoid places like this; they revved up trains of thought that I didn't want to be on. Odile reappeared and thrust a mug of something hot and pale that smelled like piss and lavender under my nose.

I smiled and took the mug. 'Thanks.'

She watched me with kind, feline eyes. Like Maggie, she was wasn't afraid of unbroken eye contact. I had sometimes wondered if Maggie did this manipulatively, forcing me to open up under her gaze. I always felt guilty for thinking it.

'When do you think you'll move in?' I asked, a little more directly than I had hoped.

'I thought I'd run a few things over tonight,' she said, 'and move in properly in a week or two.'

I'm not sure why it didn't annoy me that she told me this, instead of asking. As I got to know her more, I would find that I was usually happy to follow when she told me to. I must have been so desperate to be directed. Would things have been different if my parents hadn't gone away? They would have led me in a very different direction.

I said it would be perfect for her to start moving in immediately. She asked me to email her my bank details so she could pay her share of the rent and bills. The words, so mundane, so very *un*-magical, didn't sound right coming out of her mouth, but I said yes and got out of the shop as quickly as I could, nearly taking the mug of hot lavender piss with me.

'I knew you'd love her,' said Maggie when I bumped into her around the corner on my way back to work. Perhaps she really was psychic. Perhaps she had followed me. 'I know she's a little intense, but she's really good fun, and she's going to have a really healing influence on you, I just know it.'

'Yeah, she's really nice,' I said and wondered what she meant by healing.

◆

I spent the afternoon staring at my monitor, no longer able to apply myself fully to my work. The bookshop had unsettled me, the language of it winding tightly around my insides, a string of words slicing into my guts. I remembered the articles I had read so many times in moments of masochistic curiosity. The words were so burned into me that at times it felt like I had read them in those months after my third birthday, while I waited for my new parents to find me. They were my words, they had grown with me, they had shaped me into who I was.

Sometimes I wondered when the police would be in touch regarding Owen's disappearance, but the situation had become so normal to me by then that, mostly, I didn't think about it at all.

NINE===TEEN

The sound of the key in the lock startled me. I had been expecting Odile, had put the TV on so she wouldn't find me staring blankly into silence, but for a fraction of second, I believed it was Owen at the door.

'Knock-knock!' Odile cooed, with a foot already over the threshold, keys jangling in her fist. I got up to help her bring her things in.

I'm not sure how much stuff I expected Odile to bring with her, but it was certainly more than the two straw, reusable shopping bags that she showed up with.

'Oh, I've got more!' she said when she saw my face. 'A couple more of these, anyhow. I don't really like to be tied down, you know?' And even though I had spent a great deal of my life acquiring objects I believed would enrich me, I did understand what she meant.

'I'll put the kettle on,' I said.

'Not on my account,' she said. 'Anyway, I have wine!' She pulled a bottle of red from one of the bags and plonked it down on the coffee table. I could see her fingerprints in the dust on the neck. I went to the kitchen for the corkscrew and glasses.

Odile dumped the bags in the spare room, her room, and swirled back into the living room. She was opening the bottle of wine and I was surprised to see that I was no longer holding the corkscrew or the glasses. She had this way of manipulating me that didn't feel invasive or impolite; she would just see what I was trying to do, and then before I realised, she would be doing it for me. I had always been grossly aware of my own incompetence; I was always asking people to do things for me or seeking permission for things I could do myself. But with Odile, I didn't need to be capable or pretend to be independent. Perhaps we all need more mother figures.

Odile looked around the flat and took big gulps of wine. She didn't say she loved what I had done with the place or that it was a beautiful flat, she never minced her words like that. Instead she asked, 'How long have you been here, on your own?'

'Since New Year's Day,' I said. She nodded.

'And how long was he here, before?'

'I don't know,' I said. 'Two years maybe? Two and a half?'

'It must be hard,' she said.

I wondered again how much Maggie had told her about me, about Owen, about what was happening. It was obvious that I had been living in this flat with someone else – I had said as much when she came to view it – but she clearly knew more than that. I felt like she knew more than I had told Maggie, possibly more than I knew myself. It was nice to feel my responsibility shift over to her. I had moved straight from my parents to Owen and I had never needed to be responsible for anything other than my own past before. I felt I was, once again, being rescued.

All I said was, 'Yeah, it is.'

Odile topped up my glass nearly every time I took a sip; the bottle disappeared quickly. I felt a little tipsy while at the same time feeling as if I had not drunk a drop. We didn't talk a lot at first but there was something so comforting about her presence. I still felt awkward with silence, felt that I needed to please her. So, I asked her about her family. She was an only child, her parents, dead. I asked about friends. She had lots from the bookshop, from her yoga classes, from the spiritual church where she had met Maggie.

'She's tried to take me to that church,' I told her. Odile smiled. I couldn't tell if she expected me to say more, so I did, just to be safe. 'It weirds me out,' I said.

I had created a version of myself that dismissed anything vaguely spiritual as nonsense. But this was far from how I truly felt. I longed to find a deeper understanding, to find a way to make it all seem bearable, a grip on the world that would allow me to live as everyone else seemed to: with purpose. I had spent my teens hovering at the edges of organised religion; smoking in church graveyards, waiting for God to find me. But I wasn't found. I don't suppose anyone is. And although I longed for this feeling of something greater than me, I couldn't go with Maggie to her spiritualist church where the language and the symbolism churned up the secret that I was so desperate to keep. So, I did what I always did when I felt uncomfortable and out of place: I dismissed the things that frightened me, made fun of them.

I looked through the bags when Odile had gone. One was full of fabric and smelled like incense. I pushed a few of what I assumed were dresses out of the way and pulled out a pair of navy-blue lacy knickers with sagging elastic and a bleach stain. I buried them back in the bag and started looking through the other one. I suppose I had expected that she would come laden with dreamcatchers and macramé and dozens of strings of beads, and although I wasn't far off, there was something eerily specific about items she did bring: one red candle, a small bottle of patchouli oil, a black gemstone of some sort, a couple of pieces of chalk, a ball of string, a stack of ramekins. It was like she had come prepared to cast a specific spell and had brought only what she needed to do so. There was more in the bag, but I heard the key in the lock and managed to shove everything back and leap out of the room just as she appeared in the doorway. Her smile was knowledgeable. I had no doubt that she knew I had been spying.

'I forgot I had this in the pannier,' she said, swinging the carrier bag as she crossed the room. 'Just some shower gel and things,' she explained, and I knew that she meant it was not worth looking in that bag, that I could if I wanted to, but that I was not going to find any answers in there.

I didn't look in the bag, or in any of her other bags again that night. I didn't even step back inside the room, which I was starting to understand as hers. It had been a long time since I lived with a person whose barriers I thought deserved my respect. Owen and I had understood that everything we had belonged to both of us. I left the door to Odile's room open. There was something comforting about her belongings being in the flat. No matter how creepy they were, they radiated warmth, as if there was another person there with me. It wasn't like the flat just stopped being haunted, but it was starting to come to life.

TVVENTY

Jean was being kind, and although she was far more tolerable of late, her sympathy was frustrating. I couldn't understand what she thought was wrong with me. Didn't she believe that I could just walk out of there, with no other job lined up, and never look back? Perhaps she was jealous. Perhaps she was right.

I scrolled through documents pretending to be busy. I was trying to work out my notice period without making a fuss. I had a bit of money saved up and now I had rent coming in from Odile, but a little extra cash couldn't hurt. I didn't plan to get another job soon.

I opened a list I had made of things I liked to do. I had made the list a few weeks after Owen started at the workspace. It had been so long since I had felt so lonely. I couldn't remember what I was like before, if there had ever been anything to distinguish me from anybody else. The thing about being single that I had never really considered was that you were expected to have a personality, hobbies, a means of success. I wasn't single, but for those last few months with Owen, I had felt that I might as well have been. I had spent my whole life running away from myself. I had never paused to consider what happiness meant outside of pure survival. Being a girlfriend wasn't enough any more. I had to try to construct a personality out of things I thought I might enjoy. The list was pathetic: reading; writing (a lie, I hadn't written in years); video games (I barely played, but still I would tell everyone that I loved the way a video game could block out the entire world, a sort of sensory deprivation); crochet (although I could only make ugly granny square blankets, I tried to kid myself that this was a creative outlet); cycling (as if).

I became aware of someone standing over me. I clicked onto another tab and looked up to see Jean leering over me.

'Are you okay?' she asked. I wondered if she had seen the list, but I pushed the thought from my mind. It didn't matter.

'Yeah, sure,' I said.

'I'm going out for lunch, want me to get you anything?'

I shook my head, looked back at my screen. Time passed. I don't know how long, but when I looked up again Jean was still looming over me. This had been happening a lot lately. I kept slipping out of myself, and when I came back in there was always someone looking at me or asking if I was okay or yelling at me to watch where I was going.

'You know, you don't look great,' she said. 'I'm going to bring you a sandwich, you need to eat something.'

I nodded. I had learned that sometimes it was easier to accept the help you didn't want, to give other people a sense of purpose.

Jean brought me a cheap cheese and pickle sandwich, a packet of cheese and onion crisps and a bottle of Fanta. I wanted to be repulsed by her choices, but the sugar and salt felt good on my tongue; comfortable and cosy and safe. It reminded me of being off school sick, my mum bringing me bland sandwiches and Lucozade to aid my recovery.

The afternoon trickled by and I tried to relax into it. But every time I started to do something, panic would burst into my heart and lungs. I had the feeling that everything was coming to a head, exacerbated by the notion of having to do work. I wanted so much to make something of myself, but every time I tried to put in the effort, I just dragged myself back down.

I didn't notice the anxiety creeping back in until it hit me full force. I had been slowly unravelling, but I hadn't noticed until that afternoon at work when I realised I had come undone. I had been feeling so good about myself since absorbing Owen, curious and excited to meet the person I was allowing myself to become. I knew it wasn't normal, but when I was able to push that thought out of my mind I had noticed so much more *colour* in the world, so much more compassion for myself. It hadn't lasted long, but the anxiety that hit me now was so much worse in light of the comfort I had taken from Owen.

I passed the afternoon at work drinking tea. I had learned long ago that it was difficult to cry and drink at the same time. A drop of sweat plopped into the teacup. My fingers grazed the tender spot on my head where I would later hit myself with the heel of my palm as I sat in the toilet cubicle, using the pain to soothe myself.

◆

Odile moved in gradually, dragging fragments of her past into her soon-to-be present. I had no idea where she was sleeping in the meantime. It was a week after she moved her final bags in that she started sleeping in the flat. I never asked her where she had spent that week without any of her belongings.

The night after she had dropped off the first few bags, she arrived with a tiny suitcase on wheels. She knocked this time.

'I didn't want to frighten you,' she said when I answered, although in truth, I knew she meant that she didn't want to find me rummaging through her things again. It was this courtesy that allowed me to continue going through her belongings, although I would always wait an hour or two after she left to do so.

A surprising proportion of the things that Odile brought with her – nearly everything, in fact – was practical: a cardboard box of coat hangers; a plastic tub of toiletries from The Body Shop; a box of kitchenware with two of everything, as if she had lived with another person, and taken with her everything they had shared, as well as all the inevitable duplicates from their coupling.

I didn't want to admit to myself that I was disappointed. Odile's belongings held hope for me from the moment I started rummaging through them, although initially, my hope had taken the form of a funny anecdote to tell Natalie, if she ever spoke to me again. I had always tried to think of my life anecdotally, which occasionally helped to make the mundane feel interesting, but typically made me realise how little of my daily life was worth sharing.

The idea of Odile's hippy lifestyle had appealed to me. As much as I had scoffed internally at the fashion of Maggie's bohemian cliché, there was something in it that I felt I could use. Maybe somewhere there was a personality for me to carve out. Perhaps I could battle my past and become passionate about

Wicca, or occult philosophy. Tarot or palm-reading could be a good party trick. As much as I had snubbed this lifestyle, the few women I knew who moved in these circles were open and effervescent with a non-threatening, genuine confidence that had never seemed available to a woman like me, a confidence that I alternately felt entitled to and unworthy of.

I started making small changes to see how it felt. I went to the organic deli and bought oat milk, recycled toilet paper, lentil flour pasta and coconut yoghurt. I bought jasmine tea and Darjeeling and lapsang souchong. I cleared the shelf above the toaster, throwing away old pots of Marmite and peanut butter to make space for the new teas, coconut oil and mason jars that I filled with seeds and dried beans. I thought about buying incense, but it seemed disingenuous, a step too far. Perhaps it was because of this effort that Odile's ordinariness – which was drip fed to me – stung; or perhaps it was the realisation that my new saviour would leave me, much as all my past saviours had done: the same.

◆

I had just about given up on Odile's exotic and mysterious influence when she came home one night with two bottles of wine. We had not drunk together, had seen little of each other, since the night she first started moving in, and I was grateful to her for making the effort to spend time with me. She let herself in with her key, and I fumbled for the remote to switch off the property show I was watching before she noticed. I couldn't imagine her being impressed with my ambition of home ownership in a city riddled with housing inequality. She shuffled the bottles of wine onto the coffee table as if she were gently putting down two toddlers. Chunks of amethyst and rose quartz knocked on my teeth as she bent down to hug me. She asked if she could smoke on the balcony – 'I'm gasping' – and I told her to smoke inside, even though Owen and I had always gone out, and I had not dared smoke inside since he had gone. Odile fished in her bag, pulling out papers and loose filters covered in dust.

'What was his name?' Odile had somehow formed a smile that was both gently teasing and encouragingly sympathetic. I wasn't sure how I felt about her use of the past tense, but I told her Owen's name anyway.

'What happened?' she asked, her head jolting to one side as if to empty her ear.

'I'm not sure,' I said, and then after a pause I added, 'I'm not sure anyone would believe me.'

Odile smiled and patted my hand. She got up and walked into the kitchen without saying a word. I heard the clattering of cutlery and slamming of drawers. She returned with a corkscrew and two old Nutella jars that Owen and I had used as wine glasses when no one else was around. I wondered how she knew; we had not used them last time. She stabbed the corkscrew through the foil of the wine bottle and twisted it around so that it resembled a little stick man holding his arms up in mercy. She squeezed the arms down and pulled the cork out with a soft pop.

'A few years ago—' Odile paused to pass me a hefty glass of wine, '—someone very important to me disappeared.'

Her eyes were looking in the direction of the wine she was pouring, but they were unfocused. She shook her head gently, as if to say, *no*.

'Just like that. I'd seen her every day for seven years, and then she was gone.'

I nodded, and although I had no idea what she was trying to get at, I leaned closer. She was about to say something important.

'Sometimes, weird things happen. And instead of really processing them, people get scared. They try to forget, so they can move on.' She took a drag of her cigarette. 'But there's some things you just can't forget.'

Odile looked into my eyes and something shifted between us. We sat there for a minute, maybe longer, eyes locked. She had a hold over me, but I didn't feel trapped or scared; it was more like I was swaddled and safe. She broke eye contact and I took three big gulps of wine and put the empty glass down firmly. I opened my mouth and it all came tumbling out.

Odile nodded sympathetically throughout, punctuating my story with soft grunts, *hmms* and *ahs*. When I finished, she sat back in her chair and crossed her legs. I was shaking, and I struggled to light another cigarette. She filled my glass and handed it to me.

'You can feel him?' she asked.

'I could,' I said.

'And what did he feel like?'

'At first, I thought I could feel his thoughts. I couldn't hear them in words, but I felt I could understand him somehow. And then for a while it was... well, it was wonderful. It was like everything I had ever loved about him was mine now, really mine, like I had taken on all his best characteristics. I didn't feel bad about it. I felt, I don't know, stronger?' I fumbled. 'More confident, maybe. But now, it's like he's faded, or rather, that every part of him has been absorbed into me. I feel like I've completely consumed him and like... he's haunting me?' Odile nodded.

'So, you felt stronger without him?'

'No, I felt stronger *with* him, as if I had taken what made him better than me and made it mine.'

'You think he's better than you?' Odile raised her eyebrows.

'Not in, like, some important existential way, but he was always more successful, happier I suppose, more comfortable with himself.'

Odile nodded. 'So, are you happy now?'

I thought about this. It was true that I had experienced a kind of enlightenment, but how could I know if it was really happiness when there was no benchmark?

'I don't know,' I said. Odile had waited patiently for my answer. I felt like I owed her a good one. 'I could have been. Like, it was really good for a while. But now it's just... well, it's just not right, is it?'

'What isn't right?' she asked with a kind smile.

'Taking him away,' I said.

'Do you want to set him free?' she asked.

'I don't know,' I said. 'I think I have to give him his life back, but I don't know how.'

'I've got an idea,' she said.

TWENTY-ONE

Odile described herself as 'essentially a Dianic Wiccan', although as a 'general neopagan spiritualist' she also understood and practised rituals from Thelema, Theosophy and traditional Gardnerian Wicca. There were a lot of words I didn't understand but I smiled and nodded, and Odile was gracious enough not to call me up on it.

It should have come as no surprise when I found an occult encyclopaedia outside my bedroom door the following morning. My head was mushy, my brain sloshing around in wine, and for a second I forgot that Odile had moved in. I gasped in horror at the sight of the thick book. Odile popped up from the sofa and chirped, 'Good morning!' in overly saccharine birdsong. I smiled, picked up the book, threw it onto my bed with unconsidered disrespect and went into the bathroom.

I felt both changed and unchanged having once again

shared most of my story. I had neglected to mention my birth parents and my vague suspicion of their potential involvement in the absorbing. Odile had not asked about my past, but I felt like maybe I still owed her an explanation. I couldn't bring myself to speak about the secret I had been hiding my whole life. She had said that she had an idea, but what did I want her idea to result in?

I turned the shower on and sat down on the bathroom floor, my legs crossed. I positioned my head above the toilet bowl and threw up with all the dignity I could muster, so that the vomit would splatter against the porcelain without disturbing Odile. Waves of red rushed out of me and streamed down the sides of the toilet bowl, snaking rivulets around the grey chunks that had adhered themselves to the porcelain. After a few minutes of this, and a few more of mostly silent dry heaving, I rested my elbows on the toilet seat and propped my head up with my hands. I tilted my chin down and let saliva and bile drain from my mouth soundlessly. I flushed, washed my hands, and took my toothbrush into the shower.

Back in my room, wrapped in two towels, I felt like something had changed. Had I purged myself of Owen? The red vomit his blood, the pale grey chunks his flesh. I considered how I would feel if I had. It would be a shame if he had been reduced to this, but would it be worth it for everything that I had gained?

I swung my legs onto the bed and the cold spine of the book nudged my calf. I picked it up and leaned back against the headboard, dropping the book across my knees. It was not exciting-looking; it bore the logo of a well-known publisher and featured questionable artwork. The front cover used five different fonts, at least. I thought that the occult did not belong in the mainstream. But here it was, on my lap.

I flipped open the cover and scanned the contents, which contained many of the words that Odile had used the night before, many of the words that I had seen pasted on the shelves of the bookshop where she worked. Skimming over the section on Wicca, I learned that the religion had been founded by a man, and that Odile had chosen the most female-driven faction. I felt comforted by the notion that I could carve a personality, possibly even a religion, out of a feminist identity that I had failed over and over.

I flipped through the book for a while, half reading and half reflecting on what I thought I had learned. I knew what I had to do. I put the book down and got dressed. I opened my bedroom door and asked Odile, 'When do you want to do it?'

◆

The point of the ritual was to 'reclaim myself', Odile said.

'It's sort of a healing ritual, certainly a cleansing.'

'What about Owen?' I asked. 'What will happen to him?'

'Well, in theory, he'll be able to reclaim himself too,' she said, 'although I can't really find a ritual for this exact situation.'

She must have seen the light in my eyes when she mentioned his reclamation, because she said, 'I think we can free him, but I wouldn't expect to see him again.'

'And what about me? Will I change?'

'Only if you want to.'

I hadn't really considered the life I had taken away from Owen. He had been making something of himself and I had taken it for my own. I knew that, if I could, setting him free was the right thing to do, but I had gained so much from his imprisonment. I had somewhat covered my tracks with the story I had been telling. I'd even made a new email address for him, notifying his clients that he needed to terminate his contracts due to personal commitments. I'd tried calling Philippa to offload the responsibility, but she hadn't answered. Soon enough, someone would demand a real explanation.

Odile wanted to do the ritual immediately. She had consulted her lunar calendar and decided that the following morning would be the best time.

'Shouldn't we do it at night?' I asked, only half joking.

'Well, I'd rather do it when we have the power of the sun on our side,' she said, and I let it slide. She didn't seem as excited as I had expected when I agreed to the ritual. Instead, she seemed relieved, as if she really believed this was necessary for my soul, maybe even for Owen's. I was terrified, but I felt I was ultimately making the right decision. For the first time in my life, I was going to help someone else find their freedom, at the expense of my own well-being. *It's what Owen would do*, I told myself.

◆

I felt both light and heavy on the cusp of a revelation. I couldn't relax all day. Odile loafed on the sofa until lunchtime, flicking through books and listening to the radio. I tried not to begrudge her the comfort she had clearly taken in the flat. Later in the afternoon, she went in to work at the bookshop. Before she left, she rested a heavy hand on my shoulder and said, 'This is it, Allison, it's all going to be over soon.' Her smile was warm and genuine, and in spite of everything, I believed her.

I scrubbed the bathroom for two hours: using a toothbrush to paste bleach and baking soda into the grouting; scrubbing the stained limescale on the inside of the toilet with a wire brush; spreading out the shower curtain on the floor and wiping off the mould. When I was done, I was filthy; dirt clung to sweat, and my face was streaked with tacky brown stripes. I opened the window and ran a bath. When I was fully submerged, I turned the hot tap with my toe and felt the water heat up around me as if I were a lobster in a pan.

'It's over, Owen,' I said aloud, and I heard a voice inside me say, 'I know.' I slid down until only my nose and mouth cleared the water. Into the thick, steamy air of the bathroom I whispered, 'I'm so sorry, Owen. I love you.'

When I got out, I wrapped myself up in towels – still damp from earlier – and collapsed onto my bed. I picked up my phone. I had a message from an unknown number. I opened it.

See you soon.

My muscles contracted so tightly that I thought I heard my bones crunch. My phone vibrated again in my hand; the same unknown number. I could not bear to open it, but slid my thumb to unlock the phone.

Sorry new number, meet you at the King's at 7?

I didn't know if I was relieved or not. I had forgotten that I was supposed to go out with Maggie that night. I let myself feel okay, excited almost. It was all going to be over soon, only a few more hours to go. Anyway, I would go mad if I sat in the flat all night. Odile was going to be out – at the church, she had said – and the lonely hours stretched ahead of me like a long, dark road to nowhere.

◆

'I got you a pint,' said Maggie. I felt a flash of the happiness I had been experiencing lately. I was lucky to have someone like Maggie, who did not even need to ask what drink I wanted and still got it right. I was not so alone. I would be able to rebuild my life.

'How are you feeling?' she asked.

'Better,' I said, and I meant it. 'I think I'm going to be okay.'

'Has anything else happened?' she asked. I paused.

'No,' I said. 'I just feel like I have to accept it and move on. Thanks again for sending Odile my way, I already feel much better about being in the flat.'

'How *are* you finding your new housemate?' Maggie asked, and I told her. I told her about Odile's first bag of strange ritualistic goodies, and I joked about the juxtaposition of them against her more mundane necessities. Maggie laughed at all the right points and didn't judge me for rummaging through Odile's belongings. She had never been upset by my derision of her lifestyle, which I trusted she understood was only in good humour. She had always taken me at surface level, and perhaps this was what I loved about her. With Maggie, there was no need for me to be deeper. I didn't think she was psychic, but I did trust that she could see right through me. She could understand the person I wanted to be and appreciate that in place of the person I was.

I was not worrying about the job I had just quit, or my own inadequacy. I had enough money to get by, for now, and after all this was over I would start a new life, the one I had always thought would just happen to me one day. The ritual was at the back of my mind and it sunk deeper with every drink.

I was in the bathroom when I saw that I had another message from Helena.

> **Hope you're okay. Let me know about that coffee! Hx**

I didn't hesitate before I hit reply.

**Sorry I didn't reply sooner.
Coffee sounds great.**

The exchange with Helena excited me. Was this why I had

always found her a threat? Not jealousy, but fear of my own ability to stray? Whether I was attracted to Helena herself, or simply to her lifestyle, I was unsure; but I realised that night, with complete certainty, that I would seek her out and find out for myself.

◆

It was around midnight when Maggie and I left the pub. I nuzzled her hair as I hugged her goodnight, just to see what it would feel like. My hand lingered on her lower back, knowing that all she would think was that I was drunk. It took me an hour to walk home, but I felt too good to get a taxi. The air was crisp, and with every opaque exhalation I felt I was expelling Owen and everything else within me that was not completely mine. I felt warm, in spite of the cold, and I thought about myself with a tenderness that I had rarely allowed myself before. In a few hours, all of this would be over, and I would come out of it a better person, whole. I hoped that I would see Owen again, but I didn't believe we would ever be a couple as we had. I still loved him, but I knew now that love was not about giving yourself over to someone completely. Love did not need to be a sacrifice.

Odile's bedroom door was closed when I got back, and I tried to be quiet as I navigated the living room.

TWENTY-TWO

I lay in bed and listened to Odile getting up, showering, making tea and slurping it down. I stayed huddled beneath my duvet as I listened to her moving around the flat, clanging the kitchen cupboard doors, rustling in carrier bags and mumbling incantations or singing to herself tunelessly. When the kettle was reaching the boil for the second time, I went out into the living room.

'Good morning,' I said, with a fake yawn but a genuinely cheerful disposition. Odile smiled and took another cup down from the shelf without asking. Her intuition soothed me, and I thought what a brilliant partner she would make, always anticipating what I would need before I knew I needed it; always one step ahead, ready to offer me a leg up at every hurdle. This was the kind of caring I should have offered to Owen. To me, love had always seemed slippery and hot, something exciting that was always trying to escape my grasp, something that would eventually slow and calm and crackle with warmth when it was settled. I didn't know when I had expected that to be, but I knew with absolute certainty that when it did happen, our relationship would be safe. But as I stood there, watching Odile prepare the cup of tea that I had not known I wanted and was now desperate for, I understood the unconditional support I could have given. It was the same support I wanted, that he had nearly always provided, but it had never occurred to me that I was capable of extending it to him; or that he would even want it.

And was this not what Natalie wanted from me? I hadn't known that she was up for a promotion – at least, I think I hadn't known – but I should have noticed that she was concerned about something. Thinking back, she *had* seemed a little quieter than usual, but at the time I had just assumed that she was making space for my comeback. I couldn't even think who Michael was. Had I really not asked her anything of her life? I did not deserve the luxury of self-absorption more than anyone else did.

'Are you okay?' Odile asked as she set the cup of tea down in front of me. Her voice was comforting but she didn't sound concerned. It was this tone that had led me to open up to her; I wondered how difficult it would be for me to adopt it for myself.

'Yeah,' I said, and I was, because I had realised that I already had the components of everything I had always wanted. I was thinking clearly, rationally; thinking in the way that I had always hoped I could. I wanted desperately to talk to Owen, to tell him that finally, I understood; but I also knew that I didn't need to share my feelings with him in order to validate them.

'So, what do we do?' I asked Odile. She smiled.

'Let's just have a cup of tea,' she said, so I sat on the sofa and sipped.

◆

'I want you to take a bath first,' Odile said. I wrinkled my nose and she laughed. 'It's symbolic,' she said, 'for cleansing. I'm going to run you one now, okay?'

I nodded. She steered me towards the bathroom, where she had already drawn the bath and was topping it up with extra hot water. She had placed candles around the edges of the tub. The flames reflected in the scum of oil on the water's surface. She turned the hot tap off and handed me a clean towel that I did not recognise. I looked to the rail for my own towel, but it had gone.

'How long do I need to be in here?' I asked her.

'Take your time. I wouldn't really want you in there for less than half an hour, but you need to relax, it won't help if you resent it.' I nodded as if I thought this were possible.

'Do I need to, like, meditate or something?' I asked. Odile's laugh floated down as softly as a single-ply tissue.

'Just let your mind go where it wants to,' she said, 'and every few minutes or so, just try to pull yourself back into the here and now.' She left the bathroom and closed the door. I got undressed and lowered myself into the hot water.

◆

I really had tried not to be angry when Owen quit his job. But I had focused so hard on holding myself together that I didn't notice the drops of anger squeezing out through the cracks. I was trying so hard to stop myself from saying anything bad, but I had not realised the importance of the things I *didn't* say. I didn't congratulate him or encourage him. I offered no support whatsoever. A few days after he told me he'd quit his job, he confronted me about my snippiness. I said I was upset that he hadn't talked to me about it, that he had felt he needed to make the decision alone. It must have been a lot of pressure on him, I said, and I just wanted to support him, why wouldn't he let me? When he pressed further, I told him that I felt left out, that we were supposed to be a team that made decisions like that together.

'So, I have to run everything past you?' he said. He didn't raise his voice and his tone was flat, resigned, as if he had already accepted that he was to be my prisoner.

'No!' I shouted; the aggression echoing in the space of his resigned silence. 'I just want to be a *part* of your life, not an accessory *to* it!' I said that I was happy for him and it was not the decision in itself that I was upset about, but rather the fact that he had not thought to talk to me about it. That night we talked for hours and, eventually, I talked him into thinking that the problem was his; that his need to internalise everything was damaging our relationship and making me feel crazy, that I would not be so insecure if he would only let me in. I cried, and he held me. That night we slept close even though it was hot and gluey, and he didn't insist on pulling away from me or opening the window. I knew that I had kept him, for another night at least, but I wasn't safe yet; I knew I might never be.

I did not tell him that I wasn't happy for him. I didn't say that I was jealous – not that night, anyway – and that I was afraid that his success would pull him away from me. I understood that these were not things that he wanted to hear. They were not things I wanted to feel.

◆

The water around me was cooling, and I thought that Odile probably wouldn't mind if I added a little more hot. I used my toe to manipulate the tap.

◆

I wasn't always joking when I said I wanted to kill him. I felt that by clasping my fingers too tightly around his throat, he might begin to understand how I felt. Perhaps the desperation of my love would pass through my fingertips and into his blood by osmosis. Of course, I had never wanted him to be dead – that would be unproductive – but to take his life, to possess him completely, seemed like the ultimate intimacy. I worshipped his body – he was the most beautiful man I had ever seen – but I resented it. His body was a trap, a vessel that would eventually aid his inevitable escape. Should I remove him from his physical being, he would have no means of leaving me. He would truly be mine. Wasn't that how love was supposed to feel?

I'd always thought it odd that people talked of love as something light and fluffy, a fairy-tale ending. For me, love had always been aggressive, a battle to balance wanting and being wanted. Would he be inside me now, if I had not loved with such violence? Would I change that if I could?

◆

Odile was clunking and rattling throughout the flat. I heard her get the vacuum out of the cupboard and the soft fuzz of its suction as it hoovered up the ambient echo of the bathroom.

◆

Before Owen, I was disgusted by aspects of every man I had ever met. Their ease and comfort with their bodies and the terrible things they produced had sickened me, and I had been unable to respect them in light of it.

Owen was different. He told me about his dreams, and I was truly interested, scouring them for clues about how he truly felt about me. I gulped down his breath like it was cold, fresh air and

I watched him clip his toenails as if I were watching him pluck clouds from the sky.

We spoke of how we complemented each other, and as our words began to lose their weight, our feelings grew stronger and more complicated. I told him he completed me. I knew it was stupid, it went against everything I believed in, but he, even then, was a physical part of my being. Our sex, my cradling him deep inside, was really just my way of drawing him back to me, of temporarily completing myself.

◆

I pulled the plug and stepped out of the bath. I dried myself off and put on the clean cotton bathrobe I found hanging on the bathroom door. The kitchen and bedroom doors were closed, and the living room was immaculate. Odile had vacuumed, dusted and cleared away so much junk that I barely recognised my own home. The windows were open, and the breeze washed salty sun through the room.

Odile smiled. 'Are you ready?'

TWENTY-THREE

'I've set up an altar,' Odile said, gesturing towards the coffee table. I almost laughed at the display: a solitary black candle; small ramekins of salt and water; incense burning from a holder remarkably similar to one that Natalie had used to mask the smell of weed as we smoked joints out of her bedroom window.

Odile's eyes followed me as I sat down on the sofa, hoping this was what she wanted from me. She smiled, and I leaned back.

'Now,' she said, taking a seat in the armchair she had positioned to face me, 'I want you to close your eyes and take a deep breath.' She took several long, exaggerated breaths and I tried to mimic her without laughing.

'Imagine yourself as a deep, white light,' Odile said, and I focused on following her breathing pattern to remind myself that this was serious. I had always had difficulty envisioning anything – imagination was not my strong point, which was why my writing career had failed to take off. I tried to see myself as the sun reflected back on burned retinas. I had tried meditation before and had given up when all I could think about was whether I was doing it right.

'Imagine the light growing from your roots,' Odile said, and I felt that I needed to somehow rewind my meditation, that I had jumped ahead prematurely.

'Feel the light rising through your calves, into your thighs, washing through your belly.' I tried to follow but I kept misplacing the light, feeling it where it was not supposed to be.

'Feel it in your heart and in your arms, feel the weightlessness of your body as you become one with the light.' She paused. I wondered if she had her eyes open. Was she looking at me? I blushed.

'Now reach out and feel the energy around you, pull it into you, see how powerful you feel?' I didn't know if I needed to literally reach my arms out and so I didn't. Odile did not correct me. Perhaps she wasn't looking.

'Now, whenever you're ready, just come back into your body slowly and open your eyes.' I kept my eyes closed for what I counted as fifteen seconds – a respectable amount of time, I thought – and opened them.

'Is that it?' I asked, not feeling any different.

'No,' Odile smiled. 'I just wanted us to be present, so we can focus on the cleansing. Allison, are you sure you want this?'

'I'm sure,' I said, and for the most part, I really was. I needed to let go of Owen in order to move forward with my life. I'm not sure I really believed in what Odile was offering, but I was willing to try.

'Okay,' she said, 'take this.' She handed me the ramekin of

salt. It was table salt, not rock salt or sea salt like I might have imagined. I recognised the ramekin as the recycled packaging of a supermarket dessert; this seemed hilarious. Odile didn't notice my bitten cheeks, she just picked up the incense and started to chant.

'Follow me,' she said, between verses, and I got up and followed her in a circle around the room as she chanted nonsense words. When we had completed a lap, she took the salt off me and handed me the water. She put the incense and salt back on the coffee table and picked up the candle. I wondered why she didn't trust me with the flames. She continued to chant, and we took another lap of the living room. She put the candle down and I followed with the ramekin of water. She nodded at the sofa and I sat where I had been. Had anything changed?

'Now, we're just going to call on the elements to help us,' she said, in the same way that my mum would tell me we were just going to call in on a neighbour on the way home from school. She handed me a piece of paper and asked me to read from it aloud. She had already memorised the words and together we invoked the elements: fire; earth; wind; water. It felt like we were teenagers playing Ouija.

After we had chanted the invocation several times, Odile held up a palm to indicate that I was to stop. She cocked her head like she was listening to something far away, but I could not hear what.

'Thank you,' she said at last, and I nearly replied before realising that she was not addressing me. She smiled. 'We're going to use fire,' she said. 'Oh, don't worry,' she added, taking in my expression, 'it's not dangerous.'

She stood up and walked over to the bookcase. She dragged her fingers over the objects that sat on it and finally she picked one up. It was an inhaler – Owen's – the pale blue plastic kind for occasional asthma attacks. He hardly ever used it, but when he did, I would feel uncomfortable that I could do nothing for him, that the small plastic device that could be used autonomously could prove so essential to his existence, in a way that I did not. I had learned the boundaries of acceptability, and knew that I could speak to no one of my romantic jealousy of a medical device.

'This is his,' Odile said and I nodded, although she had not phrased it as a question. She placed it with exaggerated tenderness into the dish with the salt. She picked up the candle.

'We burn this inhaler to cleanse ourselves of the spirit whose body it nourished,' Odile announced. For the first time, I wondered how she had learned this ritual, if melting inhalers was part of some spell book somewhere. It seemed an odd choice of items to burn. 'In this cleansing, we ask that you release Owen,' she continued, 'from where he has become lost. And we ask that you release Allison from the burden of carrying him, so that both souls can be free.' With that, Odile held the candle to the bowl and we both watched as the flame lapped at the edges of the inhaler. The blue plastic blackened and began to drip into the salt; hairs of dense black smoke wafted upwards and away. The air became thick with the acrid stench of burning plastic, but we ignored it, staring into the candle's flame.

However little I believed in the ritual, I couldn't help but feel anxious that it would work. I was both hopeful and afraid that Owen would leave me or would return to me in a medium that I was no longer certain made sense. I longed for his touch; the irritating way he would graze my thigh with his fingertips until I slapped them down, unable to stand the tickle; the warmth of his back against mine as we lay in bed looking at our phones and waiting for the snooze alarm. But as much as I wanted to feel him again, I knew now that it would not be enough.

The fire alarm knocked us from our trance, and I bounced up and over to the window, where I lifted the sash up and down repeatedly; an ineffectual attempt to waft out the smoke. Odile had put the candle down and was wafting the dead space below the fire alarm with a magazine. We both watched as something floated down from the ceiling in a sycamore spiral, grazing the candle's flame and falling to rest on the coffee table. Odile beat me to it, slapping the flames with the magazine, upsetting the ramekins to extinguish the embers. She laughed breathlessly when it was out.

'What is it?' I asked. Odile poked at the paper with a long, maroon fingernail. 'It looks like a birth certificate?' I picked up the charred sheet, shuffling it in my fingers so that I was not touching the hot edge.

'It is,' I said. 'It's mine.' The names had been blackened but I recognised it, of course, having spent so much time staring at it as a teenager, as if it might reveal something of the family I nearly had, of the person I could have been. I could not understand what it was doing here, in my flat, and not in the box file my parents thought they had hidden at the back of their wardrobe. Odile was hesitant, her face sympathetic.

'It's not my real one,' I said, to comfort her and because it was almost true. 'Let's carry on,' I said.

We didn't melt the inhaler completely – it would have taken hours, if it was even possible – but after a while, Odile said we had offered enough. We took the salt and melted plastic outside, where we buried them in the dry earth. Odile planted the candle like a flower, and once again we sat and watched the flame as the wax melted down onto the earth. It took a long time, and when it was only a puddle of wax we kicked dirt over it and sprinkled more salt on top. Odile lit a new stick of incense and waved it in an intricate pattern over the spot where the inhaler was buried.

'Do you think it worked?' I asked her.

'Absolutely,' she said.

'I don't feel any different,' I said.

Odile smiled.

TWENTY-FOUR

After the ritual, we had lunch: a leftover lentil salad with raw red onion and raisins. Owen would have been horrified – he would never eat fruit in a savoury salad – but I enjoyed the meal that Odile put down in front of me. Had I ever adopted his tastes, or was this a sign that it was over, that he was no longer inside me? Odile must have made the salad the previous day, and having spent the night in the fridge, it was so cold it hurt my teeth. I relished the pain as I shovelled lentils into my mouth and chewed. Was I really cured?

I felt different, but it was nothing like what I could have expected. I felt fuller in some way, more over-occupied than ever, as if the boyfriend I had consumed was multiplying in a kind of fucked-up mitosis. I slipped my hand into my gown and touched my stomach. Was it more rounded than before? Was the skin tauter?

I listened for Owen but heard nothing. Was he leaving me now, or was he simply fading into me? Maybe I was in the final throes of absorbing him, the edges of us blurring as I consumed him. Or maybe he really was on his way out of me; his way back to me.

◆

After lunch, Odile made me a cup of chamomile tea and told me to get into bed and rest while she cleaned up. I didn't argue. I had only been awake for a few hours, but I was completely drained. I left my bedroom door ajar, afraid to be shut off completely. I shrugged off the dressing gown and pulled the duvet over my head. The sheets felt cool and clean against my naked skin. Odile must have changed them while I bathed. I fell asleep almost immediately.

My dreams were candlelit and briny. In them, I was aware that I was chasing Owen, but I couldn't see or hear him. I followed, not quite running, not quite walking, through dim corridors with carpets as red and spongy as raw flesh. I was trying to call out to him, but my voice was strained and all that came out was a marine clicking sound that echoed around me, even when I paused, still as a wall. The corridor stopped, blocked by a round and pink mucus wall with a small cervical dimple. I clawed at the dimple with both hands, gripping its edges with my fingers and pulling it apart, squeezing parts of myself through the gap as it widened. I shoved and huffed the mucus away from my mouth. I was trying to call out again, but the clicking was getting louder and more desperate. I pushed harder, until finally I was through. I was screaming Owen's name over and over again, rubbing my face as if to remove the slime, and Odile was at my bedside holding my hand and saying, 'Shhh, it's okay, shhh.'

I had been asleep for less than five minutes. I was confused and shaking violently. It was like the time my mum woke me when I had been sleepwalking. She hadn't wanted me to piss in the kitchen bin.

The chamomile tea was still hot. Odile wrapped my hands around the warm mug, only letting go when she was certain of my grip. I looked up into her eyes with their maternal promise of unrequited love. I let myself slip back into sleep, safe as long as Odile watched over me.

◆

I slept for most of the day, sliding between abject, glistening dreams and dry, wooden wakefulness. Although I was not especially cold or hot, I felt feverish; disoriented and distorted. Odile remained faithful, bringing me glasses of cold water and mugs of hot tea that I sipped at superficially until they were taken away and replaced. Once again, I felt like a child, home from school, Odile mothering me back to health. I was aware of my nudity between the sheets but felt no shame. It was like my body was no longer mine, like I had taken on a new weight, a muscular shell to house something new growing inside me. Something that was not Owen.

Before she went to bed that night, Odile turned the radio on in the living room. She left my bedroom door open at a forty-five-degree angle, where it cut off the harsh glare of the lamp she had left on. An orange slice of dusty light and the murmuring voices of late-night radio DJs kept me company throughout the night.

My birth parents hovered at the edges of my fever dreams. But every time I tried to catch a good look at them, they faded into a mist which I sucked up in panicked breaths. I would feel them in my blood, as I had once felt Owen, and then they would ooze from my eyes and nose and back into my periphery. Each time they found a way out of me, they were smaller; and each time I sucked them back up, taking more of them into myself.

I woke up certain of something the next morning, but I had forgotten what. I lay still and squeezed my eyes shut, trying to recall the message I had received in my sleep. It wouldn't come.

But something had changed; everything was too vivid, too colourful. I had a new, alien energy, an unknown purpose. I didn't feel apprehensive or self-conscious. It was as if the days, the weeks, ahead of me, were laid out on a tightly folded piece of paper that would unravel itself to reveal predesigned outcomes over which I had no interest in taking control. I got dressed and shoved my phone into my back pocket, where it bulged from my body. I gathered my wallet and keys, cigarettes and lip balm and chewing gum and tissues, and tossed them all into my bag.

I yelled goodbye to Odile as I closed the front door behind me. I had no idea where I was going.

I was out of view of the flat when my phone vibrated. It was a direct message from Helena.

Great! How about Tuesday lunchtime?

She had included her phone number so that I would have to bridge a different medium to secure our meeting. I responded immediately, directly to her phone, suggesting a specific time and coffee shop.

Can't wait. See you soon. Hx

TWENTY-FIVE

I thought I was free of Owen's occupation, but I knew that whatever was happening wasn't over. It felt like *something* was still inside me. Was this what it felt like to be possessed? I had seen enough horror films to know that the set-up was all there.

I walked for an hour or more and ended up in a cafe garden, drinking coffee and chain-smoking, trying to grasp at the realisation I had felt so close to when I woke up. Although I had always kept the truth about my birth parents close to my chest, it had recently been haunting me more than ever. The birth certificate, the dreams of my birth parents: they had to mean something. And the fullness – if it wasn't Owen living within me, what *was* it?

And then it came to me, the idea I had been trying to grasp. Odile turning up in my life when she did, the ritual, the appearance of my birth parents in my dreams. This was no coincidence. I had always harboured vague fears that my birth parents were guilty, that maybe they *had* cursed me, or they had only had me in order to fulfil some demented satanic destiny. But what if, really, I was blessed? Maybe they *did* put a spell on me, but if that was true, it was also possible – more likely, surely? – that they were trying to protect me. Knowing that I would be taken away from them, maybe my birth parents had used their magic to set me up for life, to empower me to become the best version of myself, by whatever means necessary. Maybe Odile was in on it. She could be a friend of my birth father's, the person he had entrusted with my development after he disappeared. Maybe they had always known it would turn out like this. Maybe everything that had happened had been mapped out years before I was even born.

My phone buzzed, and the vibrations and the sight of it hopping along the picnic bench shook me from my thoughts. Karen was calling. I was supposed to be at work. I hadn't been in for a few days. I had intended to work out my notice period, but at some point I just stopped going in. This was not the first time Karen had called, but it was the first time I felt able to speak to her. A child was glaring at me from his perch a few tables over. I stared into his eyes, but he didn't look away. I answered the phone.

'Hello?'

'Allison? Oh, thank god. We've all been worried sick about you. It's Karen here. You know, from work?'

'I know who it is, Karen.'

'Yes, well. Are you okay? We haven't seen you in a few days.'

'I'm fine.'

'Oh. Well,' Karen was getting flustered. 'It's just, you were supposed to be in work and—'

'And you've been worried sick,' I said.

'Yes…'

'Thank you,' I said, and I was surprised to find I really meant it. Karen was a pain, but she was only doing her job. If I let go of my own preconceptions with her snarkiness, I could admit that her concern *did* sound genuine. I sighed. 'I'm okay, really,' I said. 'I've had some personal issues, I'm sorry I didn't talk to you. I was afraid.'

For the first time I didn't feel ashamed of my fear. I wasn't the only person who was afraid, and I didn't need to pretend to be brave.

'Oh, I'm so sorry, Allison. Listen, if you need anything…'

'I know,' I said. 'Thank you. I don't think I'm going to be able to work out my notice. I'm sure I can get a doctor's note or something.'

'There's no need,' said Karen. 'Just take care of yourself, okay, Allison?'

'You too, Karen. Thank you. For everything.'

I had always felt afraid of my employers. These people held the balance of my life in their hands. They were always ready to smash everything I had, should I fail to perform to their expectations. Now I realised that I was just being unkind. It wasn't Karen's fault I wasn't fulfilled.

I stood up to leave, feeling that I was taking great strides towards becoming my best self, my true self, when a hot knife stabbed into my stomach. I dropped back onto the bench with the force of the pain. I couldn't breathe in; air was escaping, but my lungs were unable to refill. There was another stabbing kick and this time I realised that the pain was coming from within me; a cramp with the unexpected strength and power of a gunshot. I tried to sit still, to hold my lips thin and flat, to keep the pain imperceptible to everyone but the child who still glared at me without a hint of concern.

I crossed my legs and squeezed my thighs together, lacing my fingers over my pelvis and pushing down hard. I closed my eyes and tried to flex my pelvic floor muscles, but I couldn't feel them amid the shooting pain. A hot, wet throb burned from my vulva to the pit of my stomach. It felt a bit like the cramp I had experienced in the shower on New Year's Day, only more intense, more desperate. I opened my eyes to see if I was bleeding, but my jeans were dry and clean. The only external evidence of pain was written in my body language.

I don't know how long I sat there, battling the pain, trying to hold it away from my face so that nobody would ask if they could help. I knew this wasn't a normal pain like a period cramp or a cancer. It was connected to Owen, the absorbing, the ritual, and I knew instinctively that nobody would be able to help. I pressed down against my uterus as if I were trying to squeeze it out of me. The little boy still stared; his gaze was even and uninterested. I held his eyes to distract myself. I stood up as soon as the spasming subsided, not wanting to become trapped there. The child and his father also got up to leave.

'Don't worry,' said the child, 'he's coming out now.'

'What?' I hissed. 'What did you say?'

'He's coming out,' said the boy.

'What do you mean? What do you know?' I wanted to grab him by the shoulders and shake him. I looked around to his father, but he wasn't paying attention. The boy smiled and said, 'It's going to be okay.' He ran over to his father, took his hand, and together they turned the corner and were gone.

♦

I walked around for a while, holding my belly as if cradling an unborn baby. I was terrified of the pain returning and convinced that it could not if I kept moving. It was as if the pain itself were driving me. I had no idea where I was going until I got there.

The hotel was not a grand building. Nothing about it seemed special. In fact, it was so ordinary that I failed to recognise it immediately. I struggled to remember why I had booked it in the first place. I had assumed it was my choice to stay there, but looking back, I wonder if any of the decisions leading up to this had been entirely mine.

The hotel sat in the middle of a Victorian terrace. An ugly attic box-extension peered down from the roof like a nosy neighbour. There were five or six rooms in the hotel, each adhering closely to a colour scheme. I had chosen the richest, darkest looking of the rooms, the one I thought was most evocative of risk and sex. The photos had evidently been taken several years earlier, but it was, I thought, a satisfactory take on the kind of gothic romance that seemed intense enough to draw Owen and me closer together. I had been right about that.

I stood in front of the building and looked up at the windows, each lined with an absurd block of blue or yellow or silver. Our room had been at the back. I would not be able to see it from here. I thought about going inside and then, all of sudden, I was standing at the top of the front steps with one hand extended towards the brass plate on the door. I looked back to the pavement where I had been, half expecting to see myself. I shook my head and had raised my fingertips to the door when it was flung open, almost knocking me down the steps.

Had I been to this hotel before New Year's Eve? It held a vague familiarity connected with my childhood. I remembered a holiday with my parents – the real, adopted ones – where we had stayed in a hotel like this. A man had tried to talk me. What had he said? Had he known my name? Had he told me I'd be back here? In my memory, my parents dragged me away, told me never to speak to strangers. My mother pulled me to one side and my father took off after the man.

A woman around my own age stumbled out of the hotel. She had two backpacks, one on each shoulder, and her face was ashen; pale and swollen as a soggy slice of thick white bread. She didn't notice me as she took the steps down to street level and hurried away. I turned to watch her go, and as I did, I thought to myself, *Is that me?*

The pain began to simmer and I hurried away in the direction of my flat. It would be a fifteen-minute walk on a good day, but now a thousand sharp and tiny fists were pinching and punching my uterus and pelvis. I limped, hunchbacked with my hands tucked into the waistband of my jeans. I was trying to run but my feet were so heavy that I could barely pick them up off the ground. It was like trying to run through soup, or wet sand. It wasn't busy out, but I could feel hundreds of eyes on me, dozens of wry smiles at my expense. My feet were moving of their own accord, and I watched as I tripped over my own shoe. The ground hurtled towards my face, and my hands, trapped in the waistband of my jeans, could do nothing to soften the fall. I thought I heard my skull crack as I hit the floor, but I must have imagined it. An elderly woman waddled over, asking if I was okay, her hands fussing in a cloud above me. I screamed at her with shrieking animal howls. I touched my head and face but there was no blood. People in the street stopped to look. All around me, figures started to approach, looming over to leer at the crazy lady I had become, writhing and screaming on the ground. I shrieked and hissed and pushed myself to my feet. I hobbled away, doubled over and swatting at the space around me with my hands to keep the people away.

I was soaked through when I stabbed at my front door with my keys. I was making a racket, but nobody came out to see if I was okay. I stumbled through the door and headed straight for my bedroom.

In my bedroom mirror, I saw that I was crying and sweating. I was covered in a thin layer of translucent liquid, too slimy to be sweat or tears, too plentiful to be mucus. The pain that shot through me was vicious and menstrual; lucid as it hurtled through each individual nerve. I sat on the edge of my bed and put my head between my knees. I had read somewhere that this was how you dealt with shock. Or was it just how you were supposed to sit on a crashing aeroplane? I squeezed my eyes shut as hard as I could until the black space behind my lids burst into blood and lights. I breathed and squeezed until I could move again.

I couldn't remember when I'd had my last period, but a pain like this could not just be a menstrual cramp. I folded Owen's pillow in half and squeezed it between my thighs. I took another pillow and gripped it tightly against my abdomen. I moaned and rolled and howled and shrieked through the waves of pain. I didn't consider whether Odile was in the flat or not. It did not occur to me to worry that she knew I was in pain but was not rushing to help me. All I could think was, *Why is this happening to me?*

My stomach lurched and rolled. I retched as I writhed. Between heaves, I focused on my breathing, counting the gasps to block my mind from the many avenues through which it tried to stream. Thick blood pounded in my skull. My heart issued a dull slap to my brain on every beat.

TWENTY-SIX

It was Tuesday when I woke up. The light was washed out like thin, pale smoke and I couldn't tell if it was dusk or dawn. My phone read 06:03 and I put it down before snatching it back up again to see what day it was. I had no recollection of anything from the previous evening, was uncertain if it had been light or dark when I got home. I touched my stomach and felt an almost imperceptible ache.

I cracked the bedroom door slightly, casting a slice of grey light into the blacked-out living room. Odile's bedroom door was closed. Did that mean she was here or not? I shut my door and stood in the middle of my bedroom, rubbing my stomach and struggling to recall something. My legs folded like wet noodles when I remembered my plan to meet Helena, and I flopped onto the bed. The pain struck as soon as my body hit the mattress.

My pelvic floor clenched, trying to keep the pain out or keep something else in. It felt the same as yesterday, but was more tolerable this time, like the feeling of inadequacy or loneliness; a pain that I had lived with my whole life.

I reread Helena's messages to confirm that we were meeting. The weight of the phone in my hand, the promise of a new woman to take care of me, reminded me of Natalie's email. If I cast my mind back to arbitrary points from within our friendship, I could recall specific moments of tenderness and understanding from her. She had touched upon my childhood so many times, almost always accidentally, and had dealt with it with such grace that I had never felt I owed her an explanation. I realised, in hindsight, that she had been trying to coax me through life with such subtlety that I had found her support easy to ignore. She had made good on her promises to help me with my writing by introducing Cara's poetry to her colleagues at the publishing house. I had assumed this step up would not be extended to me, but it had been offered multiple times and I had never tried to take it. I should have known that Natalie would be there for me. I didn't blame her for needing some time away from me. In the meantime, I would connect with Helena.

My new thirst for Helena didn't strike me as odd. I don't remember thinking about anything apart from how much I wanted her. I didn't know if I wanted her to fuck me or mother me; if I wanted to give her everything or take everything that she had.

◆

Since the ritual, I had become more certain that Owen had been replaced by something else growing inside me. I didn't feel cleansed; not better or worse, only different. Maybe what was growing inside me was not something physical, but a void; maybe removing Owen had torn a hole in me and now a vast emptiness grew inside. Regardless of whether the absorbing had been reversed or totally completed, the result was the same. I was stagnating.

I took a handful of paracetamol and ibuprofen and lay in bed until the light became something tangible and opaque; a light that I could trust to hold me up. The pain didn't seem to respond to the pills, but the action of taking them was comforting, as if I still had some control over my body.

I waited through the creaking sounds of Odile's mattress, through the unapologetic clang of her bedroom door opening. I waited through the silent minutes she spent in the bathroom. I waited until I heard her fill the kettle and I could hear it begin to boil. When I was certain that she would be in a receptive awakened state, I got out of bed, wrapped the mysterious ceremonial bathrobe around myself, and opened my door.

Odile had already set two mugs out on the kitchen counter.

'Good morning,' she said, 'how are we feeling today?' I found it odd, her use of the inclusive plural, and I wondered again what she knew that I didn't. I wondered if I should tell her about the pain. I wanted to ask her what had happened to me. I knew she would know, but all I said was, 'I'm okay thanks, you?'

The accusations against my birth parents had mostly been pretty typical satanic-panic bullshit, but there had been one thing that stood out, one glimmering sentence that I had clung to. I found the article on a paranormal forum. It was a scanned page from an old mystery magazine in a thread about satanic ritual abuse, posted without comment. I had found it perhaps a year before I absorbed Owen. I can still recall the stiffness of my cold thumb as I scrolled through pages of search results on my phone. When I think about the article, I can feel the pain in my coccyx; a reaction to the cold tiles of the bathroom floor at work.

At first, I had only read about my birth parents' case, but as I made my way through the literature on them, I'd moved on to the panic, and satanic abuse in general. I had been on this particular forum before, had already scoured this thread. But this post was new.

There was no date on the magazine article, but it had clearly been written years after the scandal. It referenced the death of my birth mother, the disappearance of my birth father, the fact that I had been adopted, and that I had taken on a new identity. There were quotes from 'inside sources' and 'close personal friends'. There was also a quote from a woman who claimed to have been working at the day-care centre when my birth parents were taken away.

'She is not possessed,' said the quote, 'she is pure brilliance.'

The article went on to ruminate on my whereabouts, with references to other girls my age who had experienced paranormal phenomena. How did they know that one of those girls wasn't me?

I had always assumed the quote was fake, but now I wasn't sure. Could it have been Odile who had provided the quote? Didn't her face seem familiar? Like someone I had known in a previous life?

As I tried to recall her face from my past, I was aware of Odile's voice, an indecipherable purring murmur that lulled me as I drank the bitter herbal tea she had handed me. I didn't know what flavour it was supposed to be, or whether it was part of the ritual or some new spell, but I drank it all the same. When I set the mug down, empty, on the counter, the screwdriver in my abdomen reeled. I gasped. The blood drained from my face. I doubled over, and Odile smiled with sympathy. *She knows about the pain*, I thought, but instead of confronting her, I hobbled back into my room to suffer in peace.

I rolled around on my bed, trying not to make a sound. It felt like I had been skewered through the cervix with white-hot electrical wire. I gagged like the wire was rising up in my throat. I tried to count my breaths, but I couldn't count more than two before the ragged gasps became indistinguishable from one another. I focused on my heartbeat instead, trying to count along to the rhythm with which the blood pounded against my temples like it was trying to escape.

That was when I heard it. The comforting one-two of my heartbeat was unsteady, juddering with no rhythm that I could discern. I tried to focus more closely on the calamitous pulse. It was not calamitous, as such. It was not a single pulse at all.

TWENTY-SEVEN

I was ten minutes late to meet Helena, but she wasn't there when I arrived. I ordered a flat white and sat down at a table in the darkest corner of the room. Perhaps she had already given up waiting and left. Perhaps she had forgotten about me. Perhaps she had never intended to come at all. The longing I felt for her was reminiscent of the way I used to feel about Owen, near the beginning, when I had fallen in love with him and was unsure if the feeling was mutual. The desire I felt for her was physical, like my bones would dissolve if I didn't see her.

I didn't notice Helena's arrival until she swung her Design Museum tote bag into the seat opposite me. I jumped.

'Hey!' she smiled as she pulled me into an unselfconscious hug. My body was weightless in her arms. I spread my feet to steady myself when she let go. 'Do you want anything?' she asked, and I shook my head because I didn't know what I would say if I started to speak. The minutes between her heading to the counter and returning to the table were blank, as if I now only existed in her presence.

'I'm so glad you replied,' she said when she returned. 'I've really been looking forward to this. You know, I thought you didn't really like me.' My lower lip dropped.

I hadn't expected confrontation. It hadn't crossed my mind to consider how Helena felt about me, or rather it had seemed obvious that she thought I was pathetic, Owen's silly, clingy girlfriend. I took a deep breath, ready to release the new me.

'Well, maybe you weren't wrong,' I said. Helena's face dropped fast, like it was about to slip right off her skull. She hadn't expected me to tell the truth. I pressed my lips together in an apologetic smile. 'I mean, I was kind of frightened of you, threatened I guess.'

'By me?' Helena laughed but she wasn't laughing *at* me.

'I guess I was worried that Owen liked you more than me.'

'What do you mean?' she asked, even though she must have already known.

'I guess I was… jealous.'

'There was nothing to be jealous of,' she said. 'There's nothing like that between us, trust me. Anyway, he really loves you. It's obvious.'

'He moved out,' I said.

'*What?* What happened?'

'He just left. On New Year's Day. We haven't spoken since.'

'What did he *say*?' Helena's surprise seemed genuine.

'Not a lot.' I had my story straight by then. 'He just said he didn't want to be with me any more.'

I held my breath while I waited for her to ask more questions or slather me in pity. She took a sip of her drink and sighed.

'I haven't heard from him either.' She seemed wistful and distant, as if she had just been told her own boyfriend had left her and wasn't quite sure how to deal with it yet.

'You guys were together for a while, right?' she asked.

'Ten years.'

'Wow.'

'Yeah.'

We drank in silence for a few minutes.

'You want to smoke?' she asked.

We went out into the empty garden and sat at a table beneath a shabby awning. It had started raining and the drops hammered the canvas. Helena pulled her chair a little closer to mine.

'So, you're single then,' she said.

'I guess so.'

♦

I let Helena lead the conversation away from Owen, and I was impressed with the ease and grace with which she distracted me. She talked about her art for a few minutes and then asked me if I had been doing any writing. The truth slipped out naturally. I told her I had hardly written anything for almost ten years, that what I wrote before that was really an experiment in talent (that failed immediately) and personality (in which I took longer to notice the failure). I told her about my job at the council, how I had intended to help people, but became so wrapped up in myself that I just stopped caring. I told her I quit because I had felt I needed to, but that I had nothing else lined up and I was afraid. I said I didn't know how to define myself as a person, especially since Owen had gone. I told her a lot of things, but I didn't speak for long. The words just tumbled out and Helena caught each of them with care and tact.

She smiled and said, 'Tell me about it,' but instead of waiting for me to tell her, she told me how she felt much the same. She had got into set design as a means of finessing her artistic talents while earning money, but now she had painted a series of portraits that she couldn't persuade anyone to show, let alone buy. She wasn't really into her day job, the constant struggle to have her vision taken seriously, and wondered if she would not be better off in an office perhaps, in a job with a salary and holiday pay and a physical space where she could leave her work where it belonged.

'Why don't you just do it?' I asked. 'Get an office job, I mean.'

She wrinkled her brow. 'Why?'

'Well, if you think it would be easier.'

'Sure. But it's not what I want.' She tipped the cold dregs of a long black down her strong, slender throat.

I hadn't considered that it was possible for people like Helena to feel disillusioned. She had always seemed so laid back; even now, as she opened up about her failures, she was relaxed. She didn't seem afraid that she would be unfulfilled until she died. She knew life was unfair, harboured fantasies of giving up, but she knew what she wanted, and she would never stop pursuing it.

I wondered what Helena thought we were doing here. Was she trying to befriend the girlfriend of the man she wanted, or did she really just want to be friends? The desire I felt for her grew stronger, heady and disorienting. I felt myself leaning in too close, like her body held some magnetic draw over mine. I wanted to touch her. I stared at the spot on her neck where her blood ran closest to her skin. Could I follow the beat of her heart? She noticed me looking and blushed. We had both finished our coffee. I asked if she wanted to go somewhere for something stronger.

It was warm and dark outside, still raining. The atmosphere was thick, and the sky was heavy with the threat of thunder.

'There's a place just up the road,' Helena said. 'Come on, quick!' She took my arm and we walked towards the pub.

'I'm sorry I was shitty to you,' I said.

'You weren't shitty. Don't worry.'

I didn't know what to say, so I clung on to her arm and followed her through the rain in silence.

'I know,' she said, as we walked through the door into a kitschy old pub. 'It's not really my taste either, but at least it's dry.' The bar was a big room, but there wasn't much space in it. It was packed with broken bits of rotten, old boats, mouldy typewriters and moth-eaten taxidermy. The man behind the bar had a tiny moustache, a severe haircut and a lot of tattoos.

Helena asked for an IPA and I said I'd have the same. It was what Owen would have had. I got my purse out to pay and she told me to put it away.

'You can pay next time,' she said. She wanted there to be a next time, then.

We sat at a small table in another dark corner. Helena sat close to me and pulled up a stool to rest her feet on. She was happy to take up space; she deserved to get comfortable in public.

◆

The sky was yellow and purple, and while the rain had let up a bit, fat drops still fell sporadically. After one pint with Helena, I said that I needed to go home.

'Are you sure you don't want another?' Helena asked.

'I can't, I said I'd hang out with my flatmate tonight.' It was difficult to say. I wanted to stay with Helena desperately. My guts were wriggling, like hundreds of tiny fingers were scrabbling around inside me, trying to find a way out. The pain had been quiet while I was with her, a dull memory, a whisper of an ache. But something inside me was stirring. It felt familiar, and I was afraid of what might happen if I stayed.

We were going to the same bus stop, so I couldn't tell Helena not to walk with me. She fished an umbrella from her bag and I huddled close to her in the pretence of dry comfort.

'Let's walk through the park,' she said. 'I think it's quicker.'

We walked around the park in silence. There was no one around. Rats rustled in the undergrowth by a bleak, man-made pond. Helena's coat was thick but fitted; I could feel the tension in her arm as it rubbed against mine. I brushed her hip with the back of my hand and felt her shiver. I stopped. I didn't let go of her arm. She stumbled and turned to look at me.

I knew then what I wanted, what I needed; I knew what was happening inside me and what would happen next. I understood why I had wanted to meet up with Helena, and why I should have told her we couldn't leave together, that I needed to be alone. She was everything I wanted, everything I wished I could be. She saw the hunger in my eyes. I gripped her arm tighter, so she couldn't pull away, but she didn't try. I imagined her skin bruising as I dug my fingertips through her sleeve. Her free hand floated up to her cheek, into her hair. Her lips parted. She licked them. She had not misinterpreted my desire, exactly; she just hadn't understood the depth of it.

'Allison,' she said, and my name died on her lips, floating into the clouds until it was free, and I was left unlabelled, nameless. I took a step back, and then another, slowly moving away from the path, drawing Helena with me. We crept towards the bushes. I stopped, and she took a step closer. She reached again for my name, but it was gone. Her lips hung open, ragged breath escaping between them. We were silent. I held my palm near her cheek, close enough that she could feel the warmth. She closed her eyes and pushed her face into my hand like a cat. I wrapped her hair around my fingers and tugged her to the ground. Our faces fused at the first kiss.

I absorbed Helena in one smooth movement. It wasn't like sinking this time. It felt like my body was stepping into another soul. Unlike Owen, Helena was not afraid. She gave herself to me fully, as only a woman can, I suppose.

I wondered if perhaps I was not the first person in this chain. Perhaps I had already been absorbed by someone else; something else. Perhaps the vessel that I knew as my body was really the shell of a demon that had absorbed me. It would explain my birth parents, my past, why I had only ever felt like a fragment of a person, in need of an impossible love to complete myself. Could this really have been what my birth parents wanted for me? How many people would I have to take before it was over?

TWENTY-EIGHT

The three heartbeats were slightly arrhythmical. The difference between them was almost indiscernible, like a film where the sound and picture weren't quite in sync. At first, the rhythm of my heart had only been fragmented, but after I absorbed Helena, the different beats became distinct. My heart was shadowed by a bomb and it was only a matter of time before it went off. I wouldn't be able to ignore this for long.

♦

Owen and I had been together for six or seven years when I got pregnant. We had just moved into the flat. I hadn't been taking the pill consistently. I was convinced it was driving me crazy; that I could be normal without it. But I understood the responsibility of pregnancy was mine alone. I could not bear the thought of implants or IUDs, much less discuss them with Owen.

It took me a while to notice. My period had always been fairly consistent, so I had never bothered to track it. It must have been four weeks late by the time I noticed. When I thought about it, I couldn't remember the last time I had taken the pill; it had been a long time since I followed the days marked on the packet. The half-empty blister pack sat on my bedside table gathering dust. I started taking them and waited for another two weeks before I bought a pregnancy test.

I would have expected the life growing inside me to have shown itself by that point. Something had been leeching off me for weeks without my noticing. I had always thought I would be terrified by this, but I was numb. I tried to convince myself that it was no big deal. My body was constantly generating new cells. Old ones were constantly dying. This should have been no different. I believed in choice, but I was horrified at the thought of having to exercise it.

'How could this happen?' Owen asked when I told him. 'You're on the pill, aren't you?'

I saw the flash of accusation in his eyes before he could control it. I hadn't expected him to be angry. I couldn't say anything, I just stared at him. I willed myself to cry so that he'd feel sorry for me, but I couldn't squeeze out the tears. I was so scared.

He looked down into his lap and let out a long breath. When he looked up, he was composed.

'It's okay,' he said, 'we'll sort it out.'

Of course, there was a never a question of keeping it. We'd had the conversation about kids and agreed that we wouldn't be having them. I suspected he wasn't happy with the decision, and hoped I would one day change my mind, but he never actually said that. We could probably afford it – people with less money than us supported whole families – but we were unhappy, working jobs we hated, engaged in a silent battle to keep our relationship alive as our individual hopes died.

Owen didn't come with me to the doctor. I told him he didn't need to, not for the first appointment, so he didn't. I was so angry, but I couldn't tell him. I had always been so blasé about abortion. To admit how scared I was felt like a betrayal of my politics. I had always expected Owen to know how I felt, even if it conflicted with what I said. I knew this was stereotypical crazy girlfriend behaviour, but I was reluctant to apply that label to myself back then. This was still when I thought I was different.

I didn't bother to invite Owen when I went back for the second appointment. I didn't even tell him about it. He hadn't seemed interested in the mechanics of it all, had just seemed to want it over with. It didn't occur to me that he might have been scared too. I didn't think he had the right to be; it wasn't his body.

◆

Odile's bedroom door was closed when I left my room. I thought she only closed the door when she was inside, but I hadn't heard her moving around the flat that morning. After absorbing Helena, I had spent the afternoon and evening in bed, and I hadn't heard Odile then either. I expected to be slapped by a rush of panic at the thought of her abandoning me, but I didn't really feel anything. I would miss her if she was gone, but it wasn't worth worrying about something I had no reason to believe was true.

I turned on the hot tap and filled the bath. I lowered myself into the scalding water, inch by inch. I had heard somewhere that women used to take hot baths for unwanted pregnancies. I had never believed that it would work, and I had no intention of inducing a miscarriage with my bath. Even so, I ran the water as hot as I could bear.

There was a real chance that I *was* pregnant, but I hadn't really considered this before I absorbed Helena. I couldn't recall my last period; I hadn't been paying attention. It was just like me to ignore something like this.

I watched my skin turn pink and wiped sweat out of my eyes. I tried to remember the last time Owen had interrupted a bath, pressing his fingertips against my flushed skin to create white patterns on my chest. I closed my eyes, parted my lips, and tried to remember the feeling of his cool, dry face against my hot, wet skin as he kissed me. I didn't feel his response within. Perhaps he really was free.

◆

The heating was cranked high and I was sweating as I approached the counter, but I didn't feel nervous. I hadn't cooled down after my bath, just got dressed and come straight out. The cold air hadn't penetrated my coat. The heat of the pharmacy was hard and tangible; it nearly knocked me over when I walked into it.

I didn't say anything during the purchase. I just put the box down on the counter alongside a twenty-pound note. The pharmacist and I both knew there was nothing to say. The old Allison might have tried to make some skittish small talk, or worse, a joke. But I didn't feel the need to explain myself. I wasn't afraid this time.

The pharmacist made to put the box in a discreet paper bag, but I swiped it from the counter and put it in my tote bag before she could. She placed my change down on the counter as if she were afraid to touch me. I thanked her and went next door to the off-licence for a bottle of wine and a packet of cigarettes. I punched myself in the stomach over and over to soothe the pain. I tried to be discreet, but still people stared. I stared back.

Odile was in the living room when I got home. She was listening to folk music, wearing yoga pants and limbering up against the furniture.

'Oh, I thought you were still in bed,' she said.

'No,' I said. 'I needed some fresh air,' I added, because I didn't want to push Odile further away.

'Are you okay?' she asked.

'Yes, fine.' I forced a smile.

'Right, okay. I'm just about to go out to yoga, I'll only be an hour or so. Are you sure you're okay?'

I nodded and asked if she had been in the house the night before.

'Of course! Where else would I have been?'

I said I didn't know, I just wondered. She looked a little puzzled, then she picked up her gym bag and left. That was the last time I saw her. I ditched the wine and cigarettes in my room and went into the bathroom.

I sat on the floor while I waited. The room was moist and hot, and smelled of lavender instead of the usual mould. Odile must have taken a shower while I was out.

I read the instructions, even though I knew what to do. I peed on the stick, then I put it in the dip in the sink's lip, where the soap was supposed to go, and sat on the floor.

The damp of the bath mat seeped through my jeans and my underwear. I had pissed on my hand a bit but I didn't bother to wash it. There didn't seem much point until the test was ready. I drew my knees towards my chest and held my head between them. I counted to five hundred as slowly as I could.

When I saw the little plus sign, my first feeling was regret – why hadn't I bought the multipack?

Lots of women say they 'just knew' when they were pregnant, but I doubted they had felt what I felt. I was certain that I was gestating something. I prayed that it was a baby.

TWENTY-NINE

Odile's bedroom door was shut. I opened it a crack and peeked inside. I had expected her to be there, but she wasn't. I opened the door wider and scanned the room. Her bed was messed up and a few clothes and books were strewn across the floor, but the room seemed more naked than usual, as if it were only faking occupancy. She had been spending less and less time at the flat, but I had thought she was just giving me space to sprawl out. Since the ritual, I had been spending most of my time in my room, harbouring my pain and hunger, withdrawing completely.

She wasn't back from yoga when I went to bed, although I thought I heard her come in a few hours later. I had heard her rustling around in the kitchen, the bathroom and the living room before going into her bedroom. I had heard her voice mumbling through the wall, like she was chanting. I dozed off while I tried to focus on her voice. But she wasn't there. I must have dreamed it.

◆

The waiting room would once have been a living room. It still resembled one closely, with a non-functioning electric fire in the fireplace and a wicker table plastered with magazines. The wicker table was old and cracking, and when I brushed past it on my way to sit down, my cardigan caught on a ragged piece of rattan and snagged. I had to pause to untangle myself.

It's difficult to explain the feeling of waiting to see the doctor. It almost felt routine, like I was queuing in the supermarket or waiting for the kettle to boil. Whatever was happening to me was not outside of my control. It was unlike anything I had ever felt. I liked it. I had a problem and I was getting it fixed. It was simple.

The waiting room smelled like a recently bleached library: musty and old and free of bacteria. I took a seat in the corner where the television would have been had the surgery been a home. The chairs were hard and plastic like school chairs. I picked up a magazine, but it was sticky, so I put it down again and wiped my hands on my jeans. A nurse came in and frowned at me, before calling, 'Mrs Smith?'

I had seen Mrs Smith staring at me from the corner of her eye. I was relieved when she pulled her hot gaze off me and turned her head in the direction of the nurse. She glared at me again as she pushed herself up off the chair. She had some trouble getting up and she nearly took a tumble when her wheeled walker fell out from under her. The nurse stared at me too, until Mrs Smith's squeal shook her out of it and she rushed over to help. As the nurse gently guided the elderly lady out of the room, she turned back to frown at me once more, and then whipped her head around to face in front and was gone. One of the nurse's shoes squeaked and the other made a squelching sound, and I could follow the thread of her lopsided walk down the corridor to the treatment room. I thought I could still hear it long after the door had closed.

I didn't have an appointment and I waited for around two hours until a doctor could see me. Mrs Smith had been and gone long before the receptionist called out my name and pointed down the hall without looking at me. No nurse came to collect me. The corridor was seasick green, and I wondered whether hospitals and doctors' surgeries were decorated ironically. I rapped lightly on the door – a self-imposed etiquette I knew no better than to adhere to – and pushed it open when a man's voice told me to enter. I took a seat in a squeaky brown faux-leather chair and the doctor – an older man with a kindly face – asked what he could do for me today.

'I think I'm pregnant,' I told him. He stared back at me, evenly, unsure how to react. It was not immediately clear what a pregnancy would mean to a woman like me.

'How far along are you?' he asked. I told him that I didn't know, that I had taken a test the day before and it had been positive. I told him I knew what I was going to do, and his even stare softened with sympathy without my needing to explain.

I didn't share my fear that whatever I was pregnant with might not be a baby. He already seemed uncomfortable with a situation that was very much within his realm of expertise. He referred me for an ultrasound; an appointment, he assured me, where I would have the opportunity to discuss my options. I couldn't help feeling that he was brushing me off. He asked if there was anything else he could help me with. He clearly expected me to say no, but I had to say more.

I wanted to tell him everything, but in light of his clear discomfort around a potentially unwanted pregnancy, I faltered. All I could muster was the word 'palpitations'. The doctor waited a couple of seconds and then smiled before asking me to go on.

'I've been having some irregularities with my heartbeat.' I cringed at my own eagerness to appear medically enlightened, and explained to the doctor how my heart sounded as if it had multiple beats, as if I had multiple hearts. The doctor laughed off the eccentric explanation of my symptoms, presumably dismissing me as a hysterical pregnant woman, but he still pulled out his stethoscope to listen for himself.

His patronising smirk fell to a frown as he listened to my heart for several seconds. It was clear that he heard the three beats, I could almost see his eyebrows moving in rhythm with them. He ironed out his face before he lifted his eyes back to mine, like he was trying to hide his own confusion.

'Sounds fine to me,' he said, and asked me if I drank a lot of caffeine (to which I replied I did) and did a lot of exercise (I did not). He laughed kindly and told me that I was young and healthy, but that perhaps I should lay off the coffee and take up running, or swimming. I looked at the floor and nodded.

'I'm in a lot of pain,' I said. In truth, the pain had broken when I fed it Helena. It had not gone away exactly, but had shifted into something bearable. I had been afraid that it would surface when we met, but I had felt calm when she arrived at the coffee shop, if a little distracted by my predicament. The thing inside had felt physical, but while she was there it did not want to hurt me. I could feel it wriggling, tickling me with unimaginable digits, extending parts of itself into my throat or my colon, turning to steam which warmed the space behind my eyes. It was playful. Now that I had her, it was peaceful, curled up inside me like a sleeping dog.

'Yes,' said the doctor, 'of course. What sort of pain? Cramps?'

'Sort of,' I said, 'but more severe. A lot more severe. It's like something is tearing inside me.'

'I see,' he said. 'It's perfectly normal in your situation, but the ultrasound should clear all this up. Just give them a call, I'm sure it won't be a long wait.'

He didn't offer me any painkillers. I'd caught the look in his eye when he'd asked, 'Cramps?' He didn't believe in the pain that I felt. Maybe he just thought I deserved it.

As I was getting up to leave, the doctor drew in a breath and opened his mouth as if he was about to say something else. He looked worried and I asked what was wrong.

'Why, nothing at all,' he said, and smiled after a too-long pause. 'Good luck.'

TH⊢IRTY

Absorbing Helena had affected me less dramatically than Owen. The transition was faster this time, my body acclimatising to this strange new way of growth. I didn't feel as if Helena was inside me, but I did feel that my personality had become richer and more in line with hers. I had thought I disliked Helena, that her comfort with herself must have been false. I had assumed that no woman was really okay with who she was, and disliked any woman who acted as though she was. Helena was ambitious, wanting so much more from life than what she already had, but she treated herself kindly, and although she doubted herself, she had allowed herself to be the person she was, instead of trying to be someone else. Helena would not have been frightened about an abortion and I was grateful to her for this. I felt lighter since absorbing her, freed from so many of the constraints I had put on myself. Helena didn't know where her life was going, but she was content with that. She wasn't this untouchable *cool girl*; she was a woman who believed in herself, a woman who believed she was worth the space she took up in life. Now I was able to see my own life in the same way. What I had been through was difficult and odd, but I was now equipped to deal with it. I understood that I probably wasn't abused as a child, and even if I was, it did not define me. My birth parents had been accused of something horrific, and regardless of their guilt, I could bring myself to empathise with their decisions. Odile was just a friendly woman in need of a flat. I was an absorber, perhaps the only one of my kind, but so what? It was the truth of what I was, and so I would carry it with peace and dignity.

I had always imagined Helena to be this head-in-the-clouds artsy type, but I could see now – I could *feel* – that she was deeply pragmatic and stable. She was a talented artist, I could admit this now, but her talent wasn't down to some unknowable despair. She worked hard, she had ambitions and she acted on them. Art wasn't something that just happened to you if you were sad enough, it was something you worked hard on. And if Helena had done that, then I could too.

It wasn't until I realised what I was getting from Helena that I saw what had been missing in Owen.

I'd always thought Owen was the stable one and I was the anxious one, but after I absorbed Helena, I took on a new self-confidence, something that overrode the acceptance I felt after taking Owen. He couldn't have been as content and confident as I thought he was. The underlying anxiety had been there inside me, but it wasn't just mine. We had shared it. This was a painful realisation. If only I had opened up to him about my own fears, perhaps he would have understood. We could have worked through them together, and I would not have had to absorb two people – pluck two individual lives from the world – to come to the conclusion I had just reached.

I hadn't suddenly become a ray of sunshine, but I had a handle on things. I knew everything was a mess, but I thought I could sort it out. I had everything I needed to be a real person now; the person I had always known I was supposed to be but wasn't. It was time for me to take control.

I set my laptop on the coffee table and tried again to email Natalie.

I knew that I was selfish before, but I thought I had a reason to be. I didn't realise that everyone felt this way. There's a lot I haven't told you, but that's no excuse for how I've been. I'm ready to be honest with you now. I hope it's not too late.

I know I don't deserve you in my life. You have always been there for me, and I have given you nothing. I'm so sorry, Natalie, for everything. I've changed a lot over the last few weeks (you wouldn't believe me if I told you how), and I'm ready to be the friend I should have been all these years.

I hit send without reading the email back, and waited. Natalie replied almost immediately. She said she needed some more time.

Owen had often told me he needed some time. He'd spend the night with a friend, or a weekend with his family. I would smile and nod and slowly descend into a panic, thick and black as congealed blood. For me, 'some time' always signified the end. I thought, how could you need time away from someone if you loved them? I never wanted time away from him.

I stared at the words Natalie had sent to me, and for the first time I accepted them as they were intended. Owen had needed time away from my badgering him – time away from me insisting that I loved him – in order for him to remember that he loved me, in spite of my behaviour. I saw now that he had not been rejecting me or pushing me away. People needed time to heal themselves and I had never let him have that. Helena would have been able to give Owen the time he needed, as well as the space Natalie needed within our friendship; the kind of space in which she could express herself, somewhere to expose her fears without worrying that they would destroy her.

I replied to Natalie to say I understood, that I'd give her some time, she should take as long as she needed, I would always be here from now on. I closed my emails.

My mind was clear, and I felt more in control than I had for years. Was this how Helena had felt: determined, productive, rational? I had been so wrong about the point of it all. The old Allison would have slipped into depression; I had missed out on so much. But I could see my gleaming future now, could hold it in my hand and know that something great awaited me.

I hadn't checked my bank account for some time, and when I did, I saw that Odile had deposited far too much money into my account. Did I remember her saying something about paying six months' rent in advance? It seemed as if she was moving out already, so why had she given me so much money? I made a mental note to ask her when I next saw her.

It had been a while since I'd looked at my post. Someone – Odile, I supposed – had been collecting it and piling it up on the sideboard, and I had let the pile grow, knowing that the bills would all be taken from mine and Owen's accounts automatically.

I opened Owen's post first. There were a number of bills, and all the payments had been taken. There was a bank statement and a credit card statement. He had access to more money than I had known about. I realised I would need to rearrange our finances at some point, but for now, he was still paying his way.

There was a postcard from Thailand. The note was short, but the message was clear. My parents were having a wonderful time, and they looked forward to seeing me when they got back. It was only a few weeks now. I both believed them and felt happy for them. They deserved a rest. They had rescued me once, but this time, I would learn to rescue myself.

There was also a note from Jean. It wasn't postmarked, so she must have dropped it off in person. I wondered if she had rung the bell.

Dear Allison,

I know we haven't always seen eye to eye, but – as much as it might pain you – you remind me a lot of myself at your age, and I'd like you to know that I am here for you.

I think I know now what you are going through. Darren gave me access to your email and – I hope you'll forgive me – I found something I probably shouldn't have. Allison, I know what happened when you were a child, and I need you to know, it's not your fault, and there's nothing wrong with you.

I bet you don't know that I was also adopted. I was ten when it happened, and I remember everything. I know you think I'm just some sad old lady, but given what we've both been through, I think we've both come out alright.

Please let me know if I can do anything to help. I'm sure we can get your job back if you want it, and I know I'd love to see you back.

Call me anytime,

Jean

She knew. Aside from my parents and my birth father – if he was still out there – Jean was the only person who knew about my past. The truth was out, and in Jean's hands it would be common knowledge within the week.

I wondered about the ways in which I reminded Jean of herself. Did she used to look like me, or were we both just sad? I dropped the postcard and all the other post into the recycling. Surely I was nothing like Jean. I was Helena now and I was Owen. I was Allison and I was better than ever.

And yet, Jean had been so kind to me. She had written the note and brought it in person. She was the only person left that I had treated so poorly who consistently cared. She was the only one who had seen the change in me, and she had tried. When had I ever tried?

THIRTY-ONE

I called the number the doctor had given me.

'You're lucky,' said the voice at the other end, 'we can see you this afternoon.' I wondered what he meant by lucky.

I hadn't heard of the hospital before. It wasn't that far from the flat, on a street that I was sure I had walked down at some point. I hadn't realised there was a hospital here.

It had become quite clear now that either I was pregnant, or I was disturbed, my guilt over the lives I had taken manifesting as this feeling of occupation. I was ready for the answer and primed to do whatever it took to get on with my new life.

The receptionist took my name and nodded when I gave it. His eyes flickered across my abdomen. What could he see through my coat? He indicated for me to take a seat. I was early and expected to have to wait for half an hour, probably more, but as soon as I sat down the receptionist called my name.

'The doctor can see you now,' he said, and gestured towards a corridor. I stared at him.

'Last door on the left,' he said, as if I should have known.

The doctor wasn't much older than me. He was short and broad and handsome. A wedding ring glinted through the hair on his hands. Desire ricocheted through my bones. The doctor asked me to take off my tights. I shuddered as the wanting wrapped itself around me for the first time since I had absorbed Helena. The doctor blushed and closed the curtain around me.

'I'm ready,' I called. He slipped through the curtain, and without saying anything, lifted up my shirt and started rubbing jelly over my stomach. It was happening so quickly, so impersonally.

It was obvious how much the doctor did not want to be touching me. I felt rejected. The pain flickered in response. Was I the most repulsive woman he had examined? Or was he simply terrified in the face of what was happening to me, desperate only to save himself? I tried to blink consciously, to keep my face neutral, as he shifted the probe over my belly.

'Well, you're not pregnant…' he whispered. It sounded like he hadn't quite ended the sentence, but he didn't say anything else. I don't know why he whispered. He wouldn't look at my face. He kept his eyes trained towards the screen, which was turned away from me. When he did finally look into my eyes, he shook his head, as if he had just realised I was there. What had been distracting him?

'Can I see?' I asked.

'Sure, but there's nothing to see,' he said.

He spun the monitor around to face me, and almost immediately pulled it back towards him. Did I see Owen's face, or Helena's? Or was it just empty space, expanding to consume me from the inside out?

'And you're sure there's... nothing abnormal?' I asked.

'Absolutely,' he said, 'everything looks very healthy.'

He avoided my eyes when he spoke. I looked over my shoulder to see if there was someone else there. I wondered who the person he saw lying here was. Whenever I looked in the mirror, flashes of Helena and Owen danced almost indecipherably across my face. But perhaps this was not what other people saw at all. Perhaps the doctor was making eye contact with Helena, and that was why I could not meet his eye with my own.

I shook the thought away.

'But the test, it was positive,' I said.

'It happens,' he said, 'that's why we do scans. How many tests did you take?'

'Just one.'

'Well there you go. Your GP ought to have given you another one, really.'

I thought back to the appointment with the GP, his clear discomfort, his denial of my problems, or at least, denial of his responsibility for them. I couldn't help but feel that both doctors were hiding something from me. I had felt more rational since Helena, but I couldn't stop suspicion from crawling into me.

'Everything's going to be okay,' said the doctor. He handed me a paper towel. I stared at him.

'I mean, everything *is* okay.'

He handed me some more paper towels and pulled the curtain back around the bed. I picked up my tights from the chair, where I had left them folded, gusset inwards out of habit. As I stepped into them, I noticed a blueish jelly that had seeped through my underwear and dried to a gummy crust on the fabric. Was this normal? I asked the doctor to take a look.

'Oh, that,' he said. I watched his eyes as they darted up and to the left. 'That's perfectly normal. Discharge. You're ovulating I believe?'

I was ashamed that I did not know my own body well enough to argue.

The receptionist watched me closely as I left. He was still staring when I paused outside the clinic and turned back to glare at him through the glass doors.

I texted Natalie.

I think something really weird is happening to me.

She replied,

Allison, I can't deal with this right now.

Can you ever forgive me?

I don't know.

The pain started up again after that. It ripped through me as if something was trying to get out.

I curled up on my bed and tried to think about Owen, to recall his face, the way he smelled, but nothing came to me. I got up, pressing hard into my abdomen. I staggered to the dressing table and let go of my stomach to lift the folding vanity mirror. The pain sharpened, and my hands flew to cradle it. The mirror slipped to the floor and shattered. I plucked a single shard from the puddle on the rug. I couldn't see anything of Owen or Helena in my face, no matter which way I pulled my lips or pushed my jaw. I held the shard of mirrored glass against my wrist, dragged it gently along the thickest, bluest vein, leaving only a red cat scratch in its wake. I dropped the glass on the floor and flung myself back onto my bed.

I had spent hours in this bed with Owen. We had slept, touched, had sex and fought here. We had been ill together and sweated through the sheets. We had read books side by side. We had play fought. We had cried. Or had we? Were those memories, or were they expectations, images of what I thought we should have had?

I took off my clothes, shaking as I peeled each item off my sweating, stinking skin. I gasped down sharp gulps of breath to ease the pain. I lay on top of the duvet, slick with sweat, shivering. Every hair on my body stood on end.

♦

I was woken in the middle of the night by a text message from my mum. I had started turning the volume on my phone loud before bed. It helped me to relax, knowing that I could be woken easily.

> **We're having a great time here! Thailand is beautiful, I can't believe how different it is. I don't know why we never travelled before! You should book something. Don't leave it too late like us! Hope you're doing ok, you will be honest with us, won't you? We love you so much Ali, we can't wait to see you soon xxx**

How could I respond? I *did* need them, but I could never tell them that after reading the message. *I* was the reason they had never travelled before. I'd seen pictures of my parents before they adopted me. They were good-looking, they made decent money, they owned their home. 'Having you is the best adventure we could have hoped for,' my mum said once. I knew she was trying to be kind, but it depressed me.

THIRTY-TWO

Odile's belongings continued to dwindle until there was no trace of her left in the flat. She was gone. I could find no evidence that she had ever been there at all. *Suck it up,* I told myself as I writhed around in pain.

I thought about visiting Odile at the shop. I didn't know what I wanted from her, but I was so alone. I needed her. I googled the shop, looking for opening hours or events listings – anything that could indicate Odile's whereabouts – but I found nothing. I chose to believe this was all part of Odile's grand plan to disappear, rather than the work of a shop owner who knew little to nothing about search engine optimisation. It didn't matter. There was nothing Odile could do for me now. Perhaps my birth parents *had* put a spell on me, and perhaps they had not. Maybe I was empty, but weren't we all? Whatever I was now, I was the product of all that had happened to me, of everyone I had known. It was time to accept the truth of what I was, what I had been since birth, what I would always be. The time had come to give myself over to this new life, this thick, black void that stretched from my pubic bone up to my sternum, wrapping itself around me, clutching my kidneys.

The feeling I had taken from Helena faded fast. I could recall it, was sure that I could get it back, but I was becoming overwhelmed by fear and confusion. Until that point, Odile had been a sanctuary, but now she was gone. Whatever was going to happen to me, I was going to go through it alone.

I tried to call Maggie, but the call wouldn't connect. I needed her in a way that I had never needed her before. I needed her in the way I had always thought I needed Owen. It was a physical need, my body crying out for her. It terrified me, but I couldn't stop my longing. At one point, out of desperation, I started walking to the workspace, got far enough that I could just about make out the matt black sign of the coffee shop in the distance before I crumpled to the pavement in a wave of pain. My limbs scattered like broken glass. It was a busy street, but people just stepped around me and carried on walking like I wasn't there. I scraped my arms and legs together and lay in a balled-up heap on the pavement.

'Allison?' somebody might have said, but I didn't wait around to find out. I leapt to my feet and ran. I was less fit than I had ever been, and it felt as though my shin bones would crumble, like my legs were breadsticks being mashed against the concrete. I ran all the way home. I collapsed at my front door and heaved up thick lumps of bloody-tasting bile and mucus onto the carpet. The triple heartbeat pounded against my skull. I lay on the carpet with my eyes closed and tried to think about what to do.

♦

The flat morphed, creating its own microclimate just for me. The wind howled outside but inside it was hot and wet, the air musty with my fetid breath and unwashed skin; a tropical, rotting jungle. The windows were always closed now, the air stagnant and all mine. Outside, I could see the world as it had always appeared, but the walls of the flat had darkened and calcified. The ceiling dripped. Sulphurous wafts rose from the drains.

I didn't miss Owen. The memory of my love for him was crowded, claustrophobic. Now that I was free of it, I could feel myself expanding to fit the space I had always shared in the flat; in my life; in myself.

Owen's love had never been something I accepted. It always felt like a challenge, a prize I would only receive for winning an unwinnable competition. If I could only be a little bit better, I would think, if only I was thinner or more intelligent or more ambitious, then maybe he could love me in the way I thought I needed. I thought I was seeking a love to rival my own, but had I ever really loved him? Perhaps I just hated myself. I had tried to pull him closer and closer, but really I had been creating empty space within myself; space I now needed to fill.

I had confronted Helena, this woman who stood for everything I thought I wanted to be. I had thought she was smug, too cool, but in reality she was only self-assured, pragmatic, stable: qualities that had seemed so alien to me, so fake. In absorbing Helena, I had taken all these qualities for my own. Now I had everything I needed to be the perfect friend, the perfect woman. Why wasn't it enough?

THIRTY-THREE

Jean always stayed late on Thursdays. She had an aqua-aerobics class at seven thirty, so she just waited in the office until it was time for the bus. I used to think that was sad.

The car park was pretty much empty. I recognised a couple of the cars as belonging to people who never stayed late at work, people who would certainly have abandoned their vehicles in favour of the pub. I was sure Jean would be the only person left in the office. There would be nobody around to stop me.

I stood in the blind spot, where neither the street light nor the CCTV could catch me. I pulled my hood, Owen's hood, tighter around my face and watched as the lights in the office were snuffed out, one by one.

The pain had become almost unbearable, but it calmed as I waited in the car park. I understood it now. I understood everything. I didn't make any conscious decisions about what I was going to do, I just let my body guide me, pure and animal.

Jean appeared, silhouetted in the doorway. I watched her fumble to set the alarm. The lights went out and she opened the door and stepped outside. She waited in the doorway, shifting her weight from one hip to the other. She looked at her phone and put it away. I waited, spring-loaded on the balls of my feet, ready to lunge.

Minutes passed; five, then ten. Jean continued to fidget. It looked she like she was nervous about something. She kept touching her hair and pulling bits of skin from her cuticles. Did she know what was about to happen? She looked up, her gaze loaded and aimed in my direction. Had she seen me?

I didn't know what would happen when my parents returned, and I hoped that Natalie had decided to stay away from me now, at least until all this was over. Fortunately, Maggie and Odile had disappeared. If they hadn't, I might be stalking one of them instead.

The thing inside me just kept growing. I didn't know what it was, but I knew I couldn't bear it if it took over completely. If I didn't do something, it would win, and I would disappear.

Jean was the only person I had left. As I watched her, I came to understand just how important she really was. She had determination and compassion. She had experience and resilience. But most of all, she was maternal, without being a mother. It was the final pillar in the triangle of femininity as I had always imagined it: perfect girlfriend; perfect friend; perfect mother. She would make me complete.

I couldn't quite believe that this vital part I was missing had been hiding in Jean the whole time. This was the path to my resolution.

Jean approached, taking small, purposeful steps like she was picking her way across a frozen lake, testing the ice for weak spots. My stomach lurched and pain skewered me, stabbing through my scalp, right through to my toes. It felt different this time, a whole-body pain, a whole-*being* pain, anticipating this final step towards completion. Jean would satiate the thing that now resided inside me. I was so close. I braced myself. I wasn't yet sure how it was going to happen. I didn't think Jean would give herself over so easily.

I stepped out of the shadows and approached her.

'Allison?' she said, squinting and shading her eyes with her hand. 'Is that you?'

I didn't reply, just took a couple of steps closer to her.

'Oh Allison,' she said. Her face softened, and I could see the love in her eyes, the love I so desperately needed. She reached out and enveloped me in her arms.

I absorbed her instantly.

THIRTY-FOUR

The cramps intensified when I got home. Taking Jean should have quenched the pain, but it had only made it worse.

♦

Hours have passed, maybe even days. The cramps come in bursts now; small explosions in my pelvis. I'm at the edge of something but it hurts too much to think about what. I can see the sparks reflected in my eyelids. I pant and sweat but there is no one to cheer me on, no one to help me to breathe through this pain. I am lying on my bed, naked and slick. I run my fingers gently over my vulva. I check for blood but there is none. The pain is so extreme I can't believe there is no wound. I ride the pain and it feels like I am moving, like I am being thrown around. I feel beaten, my bones weaken. My muscles loosen, and my body gives up the fight. It writhes blindly, my muscles limp, my limbs floppy. It is like I am watching it happen to someone else, but the pain is mine.

Hot white pain shoots from my groin to my lower back. What is fighting to get out? I have everything inside me now to become the perfect woman, or to birth the perfect monster. My skin stretches like latex to accommodate the wild shapes that press through. Earlier, I tried to identify a wrist, a jaw, a foot; any indication that this void inside me contained a living creature. But I can make out nothing.

The pain peaks, and even though I am trying not to push, something is fighting its way out. It is clawing at my innards, determined to pull with it what it can. It is going to get free and turn me inside out in the process.

When I think it is nearly over, my body clenching to force out this *thing*, exhausted, my head drops and the spasming stops. The pain eases. The rushing inside me slows. My skin contains me. Whatever is inside me becomes calmer, in sync with my body, part of me. I run my hands over my chest, my stomach, my pelvis. I don't fight or struggle. The process is complete. I smile and everything within me becomes still.

ACKNOWLEDGEMENTS

Thank you to my agent, Imogen Pelham, for believing in this book from the beginning, and to the teams at Influx and Dead Ink for coming together to make it happen. Thanks to Andrew, Izzy, Rebecca, Rachel, Beccy and everyone else who had to hear me ramble on about this book. Thanks to my mum for keeping me alive long enough to get here. And most of all, thanks to you for reading this weird little book. May you never be absorbed by the ones you love.

ABOUT THE AUTHOR

Kylie Whitehead is originally from rural Mid Wales and currently lives in London. *Absorbed* is her first novel.

New Ruins is a collaborative project from Dead Ink and Influx Press.

New Ruins is a paperback originals imprint focused on the porous and uncanny boundary between the edge-lands of literary and genre fiction.

New Ruins publishes books that are comfortable sitting across, within, or outside of genre labels, for readers unafraid of transgressing boundaries.

www.newruins.co.uk
@NewRuinsBooks

NEW
RUINS